I0602845

HER PREGNANT RIVAL

KAPOW SERIES, BOOK #4

RENÉE DAHLIA

Copyright © 2021 by Renée Dahlia

All rights reserved.

ISBN: 978-0-6489626-3-2

No part of this book may be reproduced in any form or by any electronic or mechanical means, including information storage and retrieval systems, without written permission from the author, except for the use of brief quotations in a book review.

HER PREGNANT RIVAL

RENÉE DAHLIA

Society expects them to be rivals, but what if the best revenge is love?

Fashion blogger JAMIE CLEVELAND only gets access to her trust fund when her father is happy with her actions. If it was just money, she'd walk away, but she desperately wants to keep her mother safe too. Obedience matters to him. When she gets pregnant, she learns that her lover Craig is married and she freaks out. Her family, especially her father, cannot find out. Desperate, she confronts Craig's wife, and they argue. All is lost until she turns up at the hospital for an appointment and Craig's ex-wife is her doctor.

When DR AMANDA AITKEN discovers her ex-husband, Craig, has been screwing a fashion blogger, she's reminded why she filed for divorce. It's one thing to believe that women shouldn't be pitted against each other when a terrible man is to blame, but it's another thing all together to see one of her husband's fuck-buddies in person. But when

Jamie arrives at the hospital for an appointment, she realises she can't let her children's half-sibling grow up alone. She invites Jamie to live with her and raise the baby along with her own two children.

Society expects them to be rivals, and neither of them expect that the best revenge on Craig is to love each other.

ABOUT THE AUTHOR

Renée Dahlia is an unabashed romance reader who loves feisty women and strong, clever men. Her books reflect this, with a side note of awkward humour. Renée has a science degree in physics. When not distracted by the characters fighting for attention in her brain, she works in the horse-racing industry doing data analysis and writing magazine articles. When she isn't reading or writing, Renée spends her time with her partner and four children, volunteers on the local cricket club committee, and is the Secretary of Romance Writers Australia.

CONTENT WARNINGS

Asshole man. Pregnancy. Domestic violence. Gaslighting. Discussions on abortion, Catholicism, weight loss.

ACKNOWLEDGMENTS

I pay my respects to the Wangal people of the Eora Nation, who are the traditional owners of the land on which this book was written.

I'd like to extend a very special thank you to Amanda Brady who named Jamie and Amanda, having bid to win the privilege in an auction. The auction raised funds to support preventative cancer treatment for fellow author KD Williamson. Thank you so much for bidding and for naming these characters.

Thank you to all the random people on the internet who commented on a Reddit post. Your comments sparked the idea for this novel, and you can see screen shots on my blog at http://www.reneedahlia.com/2020/12/23/inspired-by-a-reddit-post/.

Thank you to kahm81 for the help with the dedication for this book. I understand the continual hunt for approval and validation that will never arrive. This book is for those who understand the mirage of wanting something that isn't possible.

For all those who have exhausted themselves striving for parental approval that, in the end, was always a mirage.

1

January

Jamie cradled her pregnant stomach as she stepped out of her car. She was only twelve weeks pregnant, barely showing thanks to a tall frame and it being her first—only!—pregnancy. She never wanted to do this again. Holding her belly had already become automatic even though she'd worn a flowing sun dress to ensure her secret stayed safely away from other's views. Soon she wouldn't be able to hide her belly as it grew with the life inside. A life created from a terrible mistake. Craig. When would she learn not to do things purely to gain her father's attention?

Her best mate, Vince, had found this address and encouraged her to talk to Craig's wife about her situation but she wasn't sure it was a great idea. Being here in the plush Eastern suburbs of Sydney, only a few streets away from her childhood house, did nothing to settle the unease that made gooseflesh rise on her arms. With unsteady steps, she reminded herself she was all out of options, hence why she was here about to confess her sins to Craig's wife.

Jamie checked her lipstick in the side mirror of her car, fixed her dyed blonde hair, then walked up the short path to the front door. She raised her fist to knock on the door, then lowered it again.

"This is a bad idea." She lifted her hand again and knocked, knowing that she needed to get this over and done with. The door opened and a gorgeous woman stood with her hands crossed under her breasts. Jamie forced her gaze up to meet Craig's wife's eyes. Her brunette hair was piled up in a messy bun and she had sharp cheekbones, plump lips, and her dark brown eyes were hidden behind fine-rimmed glasses that perfectly framed her face. Wow, Craig had impeccable taste. It should've been a boost to her ego, but Jamie had always known that she was conventionally beautiful. Her mother had been a swimsuit model before her marriage, and Jamie had inherited the same looks although she dyed her brunette locks blonde. And until recently, she'd been a dutiful daughter, using her looks for her father's advantage. Seeing Craig's wife only reinforced how much she'd screwed up everything. In another world, another life, she'd call this extra flutter in her belly desire, but she couldn't let herself feel that—not in these circumstances—and it was easy to convince herself it was pure nerves.

"What is a bad idea?"

"Coming here is a bad idea." Jamie shouldn't have listened to Vince's advice. Her best friend had recently fallen in love and in the process had figured out his own terrible father issues. He'd been adamant that Jamie needed to resolve her own plight by confessing her sins to Craig's wife.

"Do I know you?"

"Um, I don't think so. Look this isn't easy, but I wanted to confess something. I'm the other woman."

"Excuse me?"

"I didn't know Craig was married; not that it's any excuse, and I'm really sorry."

The woman's mouth pinched and then she sighed. "Fucking Craig. What has my deadbeat ex done now?"

"You aren't angry at me?"

"No. Yes. Should I be?"

Jamie stared at the concrete path and her bright pink toenails peeking out of her Sergio Rossi leather sandals. "I doubt that you could summon more anger than I have disappointment in myself."

"I see."

"You do?" Jamie swallowed, and lifted her gaze slowly to face the awful truth but the woman had a bemused expression. "This is not how I expected this conversation to go."

"Would you like me to scream at you?" She raised one perfectly shaped eyebrow.

"Maybe? Would it help?" Jamie knew it would help her. Being yelled at was a language she understood, and she tensed. Ready for it.

"If I was to yell at you, it would be for being fucking silly and sleeping with my ex-husband. There's a reason he's my ex." Craig's wife spoke in a calm rational tone that

3

surprised and unbalanced Jamie. She didn't have the capacity to know what to do now, or how to react to such a lack of anger.

"Oh." It took her a moment to figure out what Craig's wife had said. Craig was divorced? She should've known better than to believe the gossip. Being here was a really bad idea and it had nothing to with Craig or her confession. Bloody Vince had steered her in the completely wrong direction, and it hurt like cramps in the bottom of her belly. She automatically started to protect her pregnancy but twisted her hands behind her back instead, so she didn't cradle her stomach and give away the worst of her situation. If she couldn't trust her only friend, then she truly did only have herself. No, that wasn't fair. Vince had stood by her when he didn't need to. He'd sacked Craig and the guilt over the tangled mess was partly why Jamie wanted to apologise. Getting sacked wasn't anything to do with her—according to Vince—but she felt like it was her fault anyway. If she hadn't… Later. She could punish herself later.

"I'm sorry."

The woman squared her shoulders and glared. "Honestly. What were you thinking? I don't want your apology. If you were foolish enough to sleep with my ex-husband, that's on you. However…" She drew out the word and Jamie's shoulders almost touched her neck as all her muscles tensed. "… I am upset that you thought it was a good idea to come here and tell me about it. What the fuck? Did you think that confessing your sins to me would help at all? I already know Craig is a cheating piece of shit. Why do you think he's my ex? In what world does it help me to meet you?"

"I'm sorry. This was a bad idea." It was selfish to even try and ask for forgiveness or whatever she'd let Vince convince her she'd achieve by coming here.

"It sure was. Go and deal with your fucked up guilt some other way. And stay away from dickhead men."

Jamie gulped. It wasn't that simple, not with her Father dictating her life. She nodded and forced herself to meet Craig's wife's gaze before she slowly turned around and walked away. Bloody Vince and his ideas of redemption. Just because he'd found love with Riley and had dealt with his daddy issues didn't mean that hers were as easily resolved. She slipped into her car, turned on the engine, and rubbed her stomach once.

"I'm so sorry, baby. Your biological father is a terrible man, and your grandfather is too. And I'm just a useless fashion blogger with no skills bar my looks." She had been told so many times that she was a useless waste of space whose only asset was her beauty that she believed it without question. Obviously, it was true. Just look at her life. She eased the car away from the curb and drove carefully towards her favourite beach. Today reinforced her loneliness. She only had herself now, and she would need to find a way to solve her own problems.

With an inelegant snort—one that no one would see or hear because she was all alone in her car—she knew that wasn't going to happen. There were too many other people involved. Walking away from her parents wasn't as easy as it might look from the outside. She had to find a way to protect her baby without compromising Mum's safety. An impossible task. A little flicker of heady warmth, as if she'd sipped hot tea too quickly, rushed to her head. Was that determination? She was so tired of protecting everyone else at great cost to herself; all she wanted was to be able to put her baby before the needs of her parents. Was it even possible?

She pulled into the carpark, grabbed her purse, and stepped out of her car. In a few strides, she stood at her favourite spot at Bondi overlooking the bright white sand beach and aqua-blue ocean with the sun glinting off the waves. The wind whipped her hair and she breathed in the summer perfumes; wattle flowers and sea salt. She pulled her phone out of her purse and took a couple of photos that she uploaded to her Instagram. #SydneySummer #beachlife #glorious

The lies came easily, and that's when she knew she'd forgive Vince for his ill-conceived idea; he was her only friend and he'd been trying to help her. She rang him and he answered quickly.

"Hey. How did it go? You went, right?"

"Vince. In what world did you think that would be a good idea?"

"One where she might understand and help? I've met Amanda several times. She's a lovely person who doesn't deserve Craig."

"None of us deserve Craig." Jamie sighed. "You know I only slept with him to appease my father. He wanted information about Kapow and there was no way I was going to abuse our friendship to get it." She should never have done it; sleeping with Craig was still a method of trying to get information for her father about his business rival. Just because she didn't go directly to Vince didn't make it any better. Probably worse, since she lied to her friend. She was a disaster.

"Jamie. We've been over this. I don't blame you for that. I know what your father is like. When we met a few years ago, you were spending a lot of time with Stu and I already knew your father was trying to get the inside word on us. Competition in the advertising industry is brutal and thrives on gossip."

"Well, I feel responsible."

"You aren't responsible for your father's choices."

"I am. I could've said no to him." Although that wouldn't protect Mum. Jamie always did as she was told— no matter how ridiculous the request—because it kept her father's temper in check.

"We both know that isn't true." Vince didn't know the whole story; no one did even though she'd heard a few rumours that skirted near the truth. She was so careful to maintain the perception that they were a happy family because it was required as part of their family image. There was nothing she wouldn't do to keep her father's fists away from Mum.

"I don't want to argue about this."

"I'm sorry it didn't work out. I really thought Amanda would have empathy for your situation."

Jamie laughed bitterly. "No. She told me there was a reason Craig was her ex and—"

"What?"

"I know. Part of me is glad that he's not married anymore because I'm not a cheater on top of all my other sins, but Craig's ex-wife made a really good point. In what world does it help her to meet me? Either she didn't know he was a cheating piece of crap and my announcement would've devastated her life, or she already knew and well … it was completely ill-advised either way."

"If that's what you thought, why didn't you just tell me no and not go?"

Because she'd been taught by years of experience to always say yes to men. "I guess I didn't think." It was a pathetic comment, and she knew that it would reinforce the perception that she was just a pretty blonde who could be manipulated. What else could she do? Let her dyed blonde grow out and her natural brunette locks return? Return… Ha, she'd never been her natural hair colour because her father liked her as a blonde just like her mother. He was so disappointed in her; firstly because she was a girl, and secondly because she dared have his hair not Mum's gorgeous blonde locks. But when she did as she was told, he was less disappointed in her, and she yearned for his approval. Not that she'd ever get it again.

"Vince, I have to go." She spoke quickly into the short pause before she blurted out anything else.

"Okay. Be careful, and please come over for dinner this week. Riley loves cooking for friends." Vince's lover Riley was a pop star and they were the cutest gay couple in their social set; arrogant Vince and creative Riley. She envied their openness. She was almost certain she was bisexual like Riley, but she'd never be allowed to explore that with her father dominating her life, so she kept those desires carefully hidden deep inside where no one could touch them. In a fantasy world, she'd be free from having to use her body for her father's gain and she'd be able to kiss whoever she wanted. Like Craig's wife. Amanda. She walked onto the beach, sank to her knees in the warm sand, and buried her face in her hands. What was she going to do now?

2

Six weeks later.

Dr Amanda Aitken clicked on the link for the files for her next patient. Jamie Cleveland; eighteen weeks pregnant and due in mid-June. Her bloods looked good, and her foetal anatomy scan results taken earlier in the day were perfect. Good, this should be a simple check up; just what she needed to finish a long day. She walked into the waiting room to call Jamie into her office. Just another day at the antenatal clinic.

"Jamie Cleveland?"

An elegant blonde stood up and walked towards her. There was something familiar about her, perhaps she was a minor celebrity, or a face on an ad on the back of a bus. She certainly had the look of a model about her—tall with stunningly long legs and shapely calves. A light blue sundress hung over her elegant frame and swished around her knees. When Amanda was younger, she would've had many thoughts about stroking the soft skin behind those knees and tracing her fingers all the way her slender thighs. Amanda blinked and turned away without really glancing at the woman's face. No pregnant woman was going to be available for Amanda's desires and for fuck's sake, she was at work. She sucked in a deep breath and painted a professional expression on her face. The door of her office closed with a quiet click and Amanda turned to face her next patient.

"I'm so sorry. I can reschedule if this is too awkward." It was her. The woman who'd arrived on her doorstep six weeks ago. The extraordinarily hot woman who'd been a momentary gift until she'd opened her mouth and removed all the pleasure of meeting her. Desire had fluttered then shrivelled and died, a sharp reflection on how empty her sex life had been for the last three years. Since she'd thrown her ex-husband out, Amanda had learned to be content with her vibrator, late at night once the kids were asleep. As a solo mum, even with Ma helping out with the kids, she didn't have time to date, and honestly after her disastrous marriage, she wasn't inclined to either. She pushed her glasses up her nose. Now wasn't the time for introspection, she had a job to do.

"You." So much for being professional.

"Hi. I can reschedule with another doctor if you want." The woman—Jamie, according to her notes—kept her gaze low. Amanda hated the way the world pitted woman against each other, expecting them to be enemies simply because they'd slept with the same man. She hated it with more passion than she hated Craig and his cheating ways. The usual hit to the gut caught her unawares; she'd had three years to get past the loss of trust and the gut wrenching disappointment that came with trusting the wrong person.

"No. It's fine. Is it Craig's baby?" Amanda had divorced him because he hadn't bothered to hide his affairs from her. When they've first married, he'd made an effort and she'd been able to convince herself that his long hours away from home were work related, but since their second child Penelope was born—another daughter—he'd become sloppy. She'd packed up the kids and walked away, knowing she was lucky to have a good job to support herself. Good fucking riddance.

"Yes. I'm sorry."

"You are certain?" Amanda's chest ached. She'd gone through a long battle via lawyers to get child support payments from Craig and now Jamie would have to do the same. Empathy made her heart hurt and she wanted to rub her breastbone. She gripped her pen tighter instead.

"Yes, I'm certain. There is no one else it could be. Since I found out, there's been no one at all."

Amanda had some admiration for Jamie. It took some balls to confront her and confess, but damn, she didn't need to have to meet anyone on the long list of Craig's messes.

"You dumped him?"

Jamie lifted her head slowly, looking at Amanda for the first time since walking into her office. "Yes. There is one thing I don't understand though. I was so careful. I was on the pill and I made sure we used a condom."

"It happens. It's rare, but no contraceptive is completely safe. The pill is 91-99 percent effective, but that reduces if you eat grapefruit regularly or if you are on other medication. You did the right thing by insisting on a condom." And not just because Craig was a cheating piece of crap who probably had a bunch of diseases. Amanda had done all the tests for everything, going slightly overboard, but that was the curse of medical training. At least she knew she was clean. She made a note to get the same run of tests ordered for Jamie.

Jamie rubbed her eyes. "I'm so sorry. This is so terribly awkward."

"You were the one who came to my house—"

"I know. My friend thought I should but as soon as I saw you, I realised it was a bad idea. I have no excuses. I really made a mess of that."

"It's alright." It wasn't really. It'd been a fuck up that had screwed with Amanda's head for a few weeks, however… "My job now is to help you with this pregnancy, and honestly unless Craig stabbed the condom with a pin, then you should've been fine."

Jamie's eyes widened and Amanda realised she shouldn't have said that. It was unprofessional to let her hatred of her ex infuse this conversation. "He would do that? Oh dear. What a damned mess."

"What's the matter?" Amanda sighed. So much for a simple appointment to end the day, although curiosity had always been her downfall and she breathed in sharply. She'd certainly wasn't bored right now.

"Um, you are going to hate me."

"Please don't pre-empt my judgement. As a doctor, I can't help you without all the information."

"I think that Craig might have done this on purpose?"

"You don't sound certain."

"I'm not certain about anything. My father wanted me to get close to Craig for business reasons." Jamie fidgeted, twisting her hands together in her lap. "It sounds terrible, but I always do what my father says because it keeps him happy and that's important because… because…" She paused.

"Yes?"

"I'd rather not say. Anyway, it's not the first time he's asked me to use my beauty for his gain. I mean, it's all I have to offer and yeah, I have to do it—"

"For the reason you don't want to say." Amanda had that familiar sinking feeling in her gut whenever she spoke to an abused woman. Shit. She would have to be very careful and follow all the protocols. This was why she became a doctor —to help people—and the protocols were designed to make sure a patient got the very best care they required. The first thing she should do is pass this case to another doctor, someone who wasn't entangled in this mess. On the other hand, it appeared Jamie trusted her…

"Why do you think Craig had something to do with the pregnancy?"

"He told me he'd read that drinking grapefruit juice was good for my skin, and he recommended it. Whenever we had lunch or dinner together, he would insist. I was too polite to say no. I had no idea it would mess with the pill. Oh God. He wanted me pregnant because he wants…" Jamie closed her eyes and Amanda knew she had to be patient. After a long silence, Jamie breathed in deep and stared at Amanda.

"Craig did this. He wants to marry me and I don't even like him… All this time, I thought my father was calling the shots, but he's been played by Craig. What am I going to do?"

Amanda needed more pieces to this puzzle, like why on earth Jamie was sleeping with Craig when she didn't like him. She understood some of the attraction; she had no time for Craig now, but it hadn't always been that way. Craig had charmed her once, enough that she'd married the fucker. It wasn't until much later that she discovered she'd been tricked by him. "Does anyone know about the pregnancy?"

"No."

"From a medical perspective, you do have another option. You can terminate the pregnancy. There is still a two week window where you can get an abortion easily."

"Excuse me?"

"Currently, your pregnancy is at eighteen weeks. Abortions prior to twenty weeks are safe and generally easy to perform and recover from. I can book you in if being not pregnant will resolve your problems."

Jamie closed her eyes, her hands still twisting in her lap.

"It's a big decision and you don't have to decide today. I can give you some information if you want."

Jamie shook her head, then opened her shimmering blue eyes again. "You are right. Not being pregnant would solve a lot of my problems. But I'm Catholic. I could never have an abortion."

Amanda tried not to roll her eyes. "Once again a religion written by men benefits them." Being around Jamie apparently messed with her usual ability to filter her comments.

All it took was one pretty face with a difficult problem, and Amanda ignored all her training and just wanted to figure out a solution.

"What do you mean?"

"I'm sorry. This is supposed to be a judgement free space and you should be free to practice any religion without me having an opinion." Or a derogatory opinion—she'd grown up with a feminist atheist mother who had been almost righteous in her views on religion and how men used it for power over women. It was a fair point. She might not be as blatantly ferocious as Ma, but she'd become a doctor in women's medicine to help other women.

"I expect you to judge me. I'm the silly blonde who got knocked up by your ex."

A giggle caught in the back of Amanda's throat, unbidden and unexpected, and slightly cruel. She swallowed down the reaction. It wasn't fair to laugh when Jamie described herself in such negative terms. "From what you say, you took every precaution and Craig did this to you."

"I don't know what to do." A few tears leaked down Jamie's cheeks and Amanda's gut twisted with irritation. Of course, she looked fucking amazing when she cried. The twist changed and tangled itself up, rolling around until a faint note of acid rose in the back of her throat. Was she jealous or flustered by an attraction? If only science could answer those complicated emotional questions with a clinical logic. One thing was true, and Amanda obviously needed the reminder. Jamie was her patient and Amanda would treat her with the same respect as any other patient.

"You don't have to decide today. Do you have a trusted friend you could talk to?"

"No. I mean, maybe?"

Amanda saw two options, as clear as if someone had written them on paper and used them as flash cards. Either she could send Jamie to another doctor and remove herself from the situation—the most professional, dispassionate option—or she could be a friend to her. She understood what Craig was like, and maybe that insight would help Jamie who was obviously in some distress. Always following the rules hadn't always worked out for her and even though it grated against her training, she found herself opening her mouth.

"Look, I realise that this is a unique situation. But I know what Craig is like. I was married to him for five years, and you can talk to me about everything. I promise I'll keep it all confidential. Doctor's oath and all that." What bullshit. Ma's voice rang in her head, "*You can lie to other people darling, but never to yourself.*" Apparently her natural curiosity overrode all good sense. Being a doctor had nothing to do with this; she was interested in Jamie because she felt empathy for her. Yeah, empathy, not desire at all. Okay, maybe she was lying to herself about that. She swallowed. At least she wasn't lying when she guaranteed confidentiality. That was one line she wouldn't cross.

3

_____

"You aren't going to like me." Jamie knew it was her weakness, but she really liked to be liked by everyone. Dr Amanda spoke very kindly to her about keeping her secrets. What no one really understood was that Jamie had been keeping this secret—living it—for so many years that she wasn't sure she could talk about it. Amanda let out a harsh sound, and Jamie flinched.

"Believe me, I already don't like you. You confronted me on the steps of my house."

"Oh?" When people jumped around in conversation like this, Jamie always felt uncertain. Weren't they talking about Jamie's secrets? What did her terrible confrontation plan have to do with that?

"Regardless, it sounds like you are having some troubles and I want to help."

"You'd help even though you don't like me?" Jamie couldn't compute that idea. She peered at the beautiful sincere doctor—Craig's wife, OMG—and tried to figure out what the heck was going on. It was like being back at school and the numbers in the maths book kept blurring into a mess that she couldn't understand. Her father, her teachers, everyone said that it was lucky she was so pretty because she really wasn't academic. She understood they meant she wasn't very smart. She sniffed and Amanda passed her a tissue.

"Yes, more fool me. Just tell me everything and I'll see what I can do."

The grumpily offered assistance was still better than anything anyone else had offered. Vince and Riley had been kind but being men who were in charge of their own lives, they didn't really understand. To be fair, she hadn't really told them the whole situation either. She hadn't told anyone. Not only had she been told never to tell, who would believe her anyway? Her father was literally a rich white man who owned a big business and knew everyone who mattered. The top of society's pile. She might not know much, but she knew the world would always believe him and not her. Jamie wiped her face with the tissue, carefully dabbing her mascara out of habit, then balled the tissue up in her fist.

Amanda touched her on the hand. "Are you alright?"

Jamie flinched at the touch but didn't jerk her hand away completely. "No. I'm really not alright at all." She let out a shaking breath. "My life is such a disaster, a complete mess, and I don't even know where to start fixing it."

Amanda squeezed her hand lightly and her eyes opened a little wider. "I'm so sorry I was rude to you at my house."

"No, it's fine. I shouldn't have done that and please don't feel bad for saying what needed to be said. You couldn't possibly have known…" She let her voice trail off and would've pressed her fingers to her eyes except Amanda's hand was still gently resting over her clenched fist and she was reluctant to move.

"We've both been badly used by the same man. I should have shown more empathy."

"And I shouldn't have thrown his bad behaviour in your face. I'm the one who is the most sorry. My actions are—"

"Okay. We are both sorry and yet, bloody Craig who caused all this mess gets away scot-free."

"Shit. Not just him, but—" Jamie choked on her father's name.

Amanda blinked. "Who?"

Jamie sighed, a deep long sigh that came from low in her lungs. "I suppose I should start at the beginning." Was she really going to do this? She didn't really know how to start; this whole secret had been caught tight in her chest for years. Amanda nodded encouragingly but didn't speak.

"I… Like, what even is the start? I feel like I've been caught up in this for ages."

"How did you meet Craig? You mentioned something about your father."

Jamie closed her eyes. "Yeah, like I said. A total mess."

"I remember when I met Craig. I'd just graduated and was having a night on the town with some girlfriends, and he was leaning on the bar. He completely charmed me with a terrible pick up line and that way he smiled that—"

"—made you feel like the only woman in the world. I know. I loved it and also hated it because I knew it wasn't real. But my father really wanted me to get close to him because Craig worked for the competitor and my father wanted the inside gossip." At the time, she'd figured there was no harm in it and the sex had been good.

"And he sent you to do his dirty work?"

Jamie cringed. "Yeah. I told you you'd hate me."

"Jesus. Give it up. I don't hate you."

"You don't?" A flicker of warmth beckoned at the edges of her breath; like a ghostly chance of hope that would disappear if she tried to reach for it.

"And don't get side tracked. Your father wanted you to get close to Craig. How close?"

"Close enough to get pregnant obviously. I'd already tried with a different employee, but Stu fell in love with someone else and that plan fell over. And there was no way I was going to put my friendship with Vince at risk."

"Hang on. Vince Cattaneo, from Kapow Advertising?"

"Yes. You know him?"

"Craig worked for him when we were married. The advertising industry is a fucked up place."

"It is?" Jamie didn't really know anything different, but the idea that other businesses didn't operate on her father's rules was kind of nice. "Whatever. Anyway, my father runs Cleveland Advertising and they've been rivals for ages, and my father doesn't know that I'm friends with Vince. I'd do anything to protect that friendship."

"Even a bit of corporate espionage?"

"Well, I mean, that makes it sound pretty dodgy." Jamie shook her head. "What am I saying? Yes it was probably that dodgy. Anyway, Vince is my mate—that's a whole other story—and I was trying to balance what my father wanted with keeping that friendship away from my father."

"I'm sorry to say this but your father sounds like a piece of work."

"Um, yes. But I don't have any choice."

"You are a grown woman. Move out."

"No, you don't understand. If I don't do what he says, then he hurts my mother." Jamie clapped her hand across her mouth. She'd never told anyone that before.

"How?"

"He threatens to hit her if I don't do what he wants." The ugly secret of her life blurted out and her mouth filled with bile. Oh no. He was going to be so angry now. She wanted to rewind, to suck those words back inside where they were safe. Where Mum was safe.

Amanda tilted her head to the side and considered Jamie for a long time before she spoke in a gentle tone. "Is it possible that your father is gaslighting you? He gets you to do his bidding by threatening to hurt your Mum." Amanda's mouth pinched tight and her eyes narrowed.

"He's what?"

"Gaslighting. It means that someone tells you things that make you question your reality. I think your father tells you that threat and it makes you do as he says, so he gains power over you without having to carry out the actual threat."

"No, yes… Maybe?" Jamie was so confused, but at least

that feeling was familiar. "I told you that you'd hate me. I'm so weak but I don't know what else to do."

"Call his bluff."

"Excuse me?"

"I think…" Amanda paused. "I think that your father is abusing you with this threat. I have no idea if there is any substance to the threat, but it's certainly working for him."

Jamie wished Amanda was right, but life never worked out so well for her. "But what if he does hurt her? Then he's right and I'm just a blonde who… well, never mind."

"You are more than the mean crap he's filled your head with."

"You can't know that." Jamie eased out a shaky breath. Maybe in another world, but she couldn't think past the idea that her father wasn't actually going to carry out his threat. That flicker of hope flashed past again, still out of reach but less vague than before. Almost graspable. Was Amanda right and Mum would be safe if she left home? Could she take that risk?

"I know that you were brave enough to confess your sins to me. Most people would have slunk away and not bothered. Yes, I was angry at you because what the hell… Craig is the one who has behaved badly, not me or you. I admire your bravery, and it tells me that you are tougher than you've been told you are."

"I wish that was true. I only went to tell you because my friend Vince told me to."

"Why would he do that?"

"He thought it would help me, and he doesn't know about my family situation."

"And did it help?" Amanda pushed her glasses up her nose, drawing attention to her gorgeous brown eyes. There was a kindness in her gaze that Jamie desired more than sex. Yeah right. If Jamie wasn't so confused by this conversation, she might have stared wantonly at her. Enjoying sex and wanting to be held by people was one of the reasons she was here, and she would be well placed to remember that.

"No. Maybe? I don't know. I hurt you and I hate that I did that, but I think it did help because it made me feel less alone. When you called him a cheating sack of effluent or whatever it was, I felt like I'd met one person who understood what this felt like." She couldn't get her head around the idea that her father's threats might not be real. If Amanda was right, then she could just leave, and Mum would be... okay? Her head started to ache at her temples. Life was a lot easier when she did as she was told.

"If it makes you feel better, you aren't the only one who has been charmed by Craig."

Jamie winced and shook her head. "It doesn't make me feel better. I wasn't charmed by him. I only did this because I thought it would keep Mum safe. If that's not true..."

"I'm so sorry."

Jamie gasped. She'd probably hurt Amanda's feelings by saying she wasn't charmed by Craig, because Amanda obviously had been at some point. "Um, hey. I meant that I felt like you understood how I felt because you were so angry at Craig and I'm so angry at my father. He pushed me into spending time with Craig for business reasons—"

"Unethical business reasons."

"I think we are a long way past ethics here."

Amanda grinned. "Very true. You are a lot cleverer than people think you are."

A hot flush spread over Jamie's skin. "You think so?" No one ever said that she was clever. Oh. Em. Gee. She wished she could believe it.

"I think a lot of people underestimate you. Anyway, I'm sorry I interrupted. You were saying that you are angry at your father for pushing you to spend time with Craig?"

"I am. I'm also really really angry at Craig. I can't believe he deliberately messed with my birth control. He did this to me, and I don't know what to do now. But I tell you one thing. I am never going to marry him."

"Why on earth would you marry him?"

Jamie scratched her forehead. Marriage hadn't been discussed and yet, she knew Craig would ask as soon as he found out about the pregnancy. Perhaps he'd planned it all along because... "I think Craig is double crossing my father."

Amanda rolled her eyes. "I'd believe that. But why try and get you pregnant?"

"I wonder... Um, if I'm pregnant, then I think Craig believes my father will force us to marry—"

"It's not the eighteenth century." Amanda snorted and Jamie wished she could smile at the joke. Instead she shook her head because her father's old fashioned Catholic values had made it too easy for Craig to get everything he wanted.

"It's all about perception management. My father likes to portray our family as perfect. Having a pregnant unmarried daughter doesn't fit his image."

"And Craig would get some advantage from this?"

"Of course. I'm an only child. Whoever I marry will eventually own my father's business. I don't know why I didn't see it before." She wanted to slap herself on the forehead because she was such a fool that she hadn't figured this out until it was too late. But what other option did she have?

4

———

Holy shit. This was some whacky old fashioned nonsense. A light flashed in Amanda's brain. Fucking hell—speaking of historically inspired ideas... She laughed, unable to stop herself.

"What is so funny?" Hurt infused Jamie's tone and Amanda gulped.

"We should get married."

"What?" Jamie blinked, appearing as stunned as Amanda felt inside.

"I think we should get married." Amanda wasn't going to lie to herself anymore. She wanted Jamie in her bed, and this whole fucking wild saga was about to give her the ultimate revenge on Craig. He'd cheated on her for their whole marriage. By marrying Jamie, Amanda would rip away his latest scheme from under his feet. His plan would fail, and she would be the reason for his failure. Joy bubbled in her throat. Revenge would taste sweet.

"I don't understand."

"It's legal in NSW now." Amanda had no idea how Jamie might react to a lesbian marriage, especially as she'd mentioned being Catholic before. Fuck—her stomach sank and she held her breath, waiting for the inevitable homophobic rejection.

"But? Why me?"

Amanda's breath hissed out slowly, grateful that Jamie didn't react badly to the whole concept. Confusion was better than bigotry any day. She paused before answering, and bit back the word 'obviously', because she'd been listening to Jamie undermine herself for the entire appointment now and if one thing was obvious it was that Jamie had no confidence in her own brain.

"If you are married, then Craig can't marry you because it's illegal to marry two people in NSW. Then his scheme fails, and he won't get your father's business."

"No, you do." Once again, Jamie proved her worth with strategic understanding.

Amanda shook her head; that wasn't why she proposed. "No. You do." She didn't want anything to do with the advertising industry—she had her own career—but she really wanted to stop Craig succeeding by nefarious means. "I want to beat Craig at his own game, and besides, I imagine your father isn't going to drop dead anytime soon." Or maybe he was frail and that was Craig's gross motivation. Fuck, she couldn't say that aloud. She gritted her teeth together to keep that thought inside.

"No. He's very healthy and only in his early sixties."

Amanda swallowed. Thank fuck for that; even assholes

28

didn't deserve to be preyed upon when unhealthy. "I reckon that means Craig was playing a long game."

"Yeah?"

"It's one that you can play too. Marry me, beat Craig, and I will help you with the pregnancy and everything."

"What do you gain from this?"

Amanda breathed out slowly. "Honestly. Revenge. I adore the idea of beating Craig with his own scheme. It's the perfect revenge for the way he's treated me." She didn't want to get into the long drawn out story of her attempts to get child support from him. "Oh my fucking God. Plus, your child is the sibling to my children and if we marry they'll all grow up together."

"You have kids? This just gets worse." Jamie bent her head and stared at her lap.

"Or it's the perfect solution. We marry, I support you, and all three children grow up together."

"And eventually you get my father's business."

Amanda couldn't imagine growing up always wondering about someone's motives. She reached out and brushed away the tear sliding down Jamie's face. "Hey, just because your father only does things that benefit him, doesn't mean that other people will do that too." Amanda placed her hand back on her desk with Jamie's tear sitting in a droplet on her end of her finger. She couldn't bring herself to wipe it away with a tissue.

"Okay. I need to think about this."

"That's fine. Take all the time you need. I don't want to run an advertising company. I couldn't think of anything worse, but something tells me that you'd be great at it."

Jamie looked up, her blue eyes awash and shining. "Why do say such things?"

"Because it's true. You are a beautiful woman who has been gaslit by a terrible man. I believe that you could achieve anything once you learn to trust yourself and believe in yourself."

"You do?"

"I do." Amanda waited but Jamie just stared at her with such longing and hope that it took all of Amanda's control not to lean forward and kiss her. She'd started this appointment with a flutter of desire and it'd grown and grown until now her skin sung with lust. Appointment. Shit. One gorgeous woman with an impossible dilemma and she'd forgotten how to be a professional. It'd been so long since she'd been hugged—fucked—by another human. Yeah, she scoffed at herself, that was totally why she was out of sorts. Nothing to do with revenge and the way that made her heart race at the possibility, and certainly nothing at all to do with Jamie, her model perfect looks, and the extraordinary puzzle surrounding her pregnancy.

Amanda wanted to scoff at herself but first she needed to actually do her job. "In terms of your appointment, I've been through your files and everything looks perfect with the baby, so please don't stress about that. I want you to know that I'm one hundred percent committed to this idea of marrying you. It'd be like an old fashioned marriage of convenience, so you don't need to worry about anything on that front."

A light blush spread over Jamie's cheeks. "I'm not saying no because I'm Catholic and stuff."

Amanda raised one eyebrow. "Hold on. You won't get an abortion because you are Catholic, but you are okay with gay marriage?"

"I don't want an abortion because I already love this baby. They move inside me and are real, and I couldn't do that. I'm not really Catholic. It's like everything in my life; just perception management."

"It's pretty neat when they start moving." Amanda realised she'd never be bored around Jamie. Her views on life were so confused, and Amanda really wanted to be there when Jamie worked out what she truly thought about everything. It'd be like watching an orchid unveil, spreading petals wide—which brought a much more erotic image to mind. Kissing Jamie would be an extra bonus in this whole scheme.

"And you said you'd support me if we marry?"

"Of course. It might be a marriage of convenience to gain revenge on a terrible man, to stop him benefitting from his cheating ways... Because trust me, the way he deliberately upset your contraceptives is him cheating his way into success." Amanda growled under her breath. "Fucking please say yes. I want to beat him so much."

"That's probably an unhealthy reason for me to agree, but I really want that too. I want to win at something for the first time in my life. And you are so pretty too."

"Excuse me?" Did she just hear that right?

"Um, nothing. Yes. Let's get married." A light pink flush spread over Jamie's cheeks, highlighting a few freckles scattered on her nose. Her blue eyes sparkled.

"You won't regret this." Amanda couldn't stop the wide

grin that broke out on her face and the joy that bubbled up in her throat, threatening to spill out. She'd gain a gorgeous wife, give a good home to her children's sibling, and kick Craig's shitty plans out from under him. Ha!

"I hope you are right."

"So do I. Let's exchange phone numbers and we can meet over coffee in a few days to work out the details."

Jamie nodded and pulled her phone out of her purse. "I'd like that. What is your number? I'll call you and you'll have mine."

Amanda gave her the number, heard her phone ring a couple of times, then smiled as Jamie stood up. "I'll see you in a few days."

Jamie put her phone back in her purse and clutched it tight against her pregnant belly. "Okay." She turned and walked elegantly out of Amanda's office but hopefully not out of her life. There was a very real chance that Jamie would think about this and decide it was a terrible idea, but for some reason—and with zero evidence—Amanda had the sense that Jamie wanted to beat Craig as much as she did. Revenge would be sweet, like sugary kisses in the sunshine. Wouldn't it?

5

Jamie reached into her green leather Kate Spade shoulder bag and wrapped her fingers around the little jeweller's box inside. She really hoped Amanda loved the ring she'd selected. If they were going to marry, then Jamie wanted to do this properly. She blew out an unsteady breath into the hot February air. Was she really going to do this? Yes. This was her way of taking back control over her life. It felt good, so good that she could convince herself that Amanda was correct when she declared that Father was faking. He wouldn't hurt Mum because Amanda had said it was a lie to keep Jamie at home where he could control her. Mum would be fine without her. She didn't really know who to believe; she wanted it to be true, that's all.

The sea breeze fluttered over the sand, slightly cooler than the summer sun, but it didn't really take the edge off the heat coursing in her veins. Part of her decision revolved around how freaking gorgeous Amanda was. She had a way of looking at Jamie as if nothing else mattered, and for once in Jamie's life it felt genuine. A rarity in her world where everyone only cared about their image, and of course, that was why Jamie had spent two whole days scouring jewellery shops for the perfect ring. One that wasn't too ostentatious; something classical, a princess diamond but with a unique setting that reflected their unusual situation. The more she'd thought about it, the more she loved the idea of choosing her own future. Kissing Amanda was high on her list of wants as well, she could imagine the softness of her lips against hers and she squeezed her thighs together. Warmth filled her core, inspired purely by lust. There was a certain thrill in making a choice that stole away control from Craig and her father; a different type of anticipation. Both lust and victory swirled together in her veins, building into a groundswell of excitement. She traced her fingers over the soft cardboard box and over the satin ribbon tying it together.

Gosh, she hoped Amanda liked the ring. The rose gold ring with three small gems in a swirl setting leading to the princess cut diamond was so aesthetically pleasing; and the choice of gems, soft pink morganite, lush blue of the topaz, and a violet sapphire with hints of chartreuse, was brilliant. She absolutely adored the way the three gems reminded her of the bisexual flag. As soon as she'd seen it, she knew it was the perfect engagement ring. She'd guessed Amanda's ring size and hoped it was correct. She'd attended so many artisan jeweller's collection openings that she ought to be quite close in her estimation. Having Amanda's hand rest on hers at the doctor's appointment helped too; the shape of Amanda's fingers was burnt onto her skin like a brand. Now she just needed Amanda to arrive at this little café.

"Would you like something?"

"No thanks. I'm waiting for a friend. We'll order when she gets here."

"Water?"

"Yes please. Sparkling would be fantastic. Thank you." Jamie forced herself to stop touching the ring box and she laid her hands on the table.

"Hello." Amanda slid into the chair opposite, looking as beautiful and contained, confident, as the two other times they'd met. Only two. The awe that filled her chest at the idea she was about to marry someone she barely knew fled when Amanda reached over and touched Jamie on the hand. Damn, she could get used to these little reassuring touches and she knew that it didn't matter that they'd only just met. They'd gone from being enemies to having a common enemy and it was only together that they'd defeat Craig's plan. When she wasn't obsessing about a ring, Jamie had spent the rest of her time figuring out what she wanted, and she'd quickly realised that Amanda had been correct. As her father's only child, she would inherit the business one day— an idea she'd never pictured before—and that gave her a specific power. Whoever she married would also own the business, and it sure as heck wouldn't be Craig. If it was going to be anyone, it would Amanda whose understated desire to seek revenge on her ex-husband had given Jamie a choice for the first time in her life. She wouldn't throw away such power on a man; she could gift it to the person who made her aware of it. Time would tell if it was a good choice. It was her choice, and that was the reason her toes tapped in her sandals and her fingertips were clammy.

"Hi. I haven't ordered yet."

"I think I'm too nervous to eat just yet."

Jamie frowned. "You don't look nervous."

Amanda shrugged. "I wasn't sure you'd be here, but now you are, I'm okay."

"I didn't think you'd come either. Your idea is too perfect to be true."

"So you will marry me? And together we can make sure Craig doesn't win his evil game."

Jamie giggled—for the first time in months—and it clung awkwardly in the air. "I got you a ring. I hope it fits." She pulled the little box out of her purse and placed it on the table with shaking fingers. Amanda opened it and gasped.

"It's perfect. So pretty and… Oh wow." Amanda slid the ring onto her finger and it fit perfectly. A smug warmth surrounded Jamie's chest—she'd picked the correct size. She might not know much, but she knew fashion. The ring sat on Amanda's elegant finger like it belonged there, making the idea of their marriage real. Jamie couldn't breathe; suddenly she wanted more than revenge. She wanted everything she'd never had—a loving family for her baby, and a partner who cared for her more than for image or business success—and she had to remind herself that this wasn't love or lust. It was simply two people with a common enemy.

"It looks good on you." Jamie forced out the polite words, while her pulse raced erratically.

"Thank you. I got you one too. Except not."

"Excuse me?" What on earth did that mean? Jamie dropped her hands to her lap and clutched her purse under the table.

"I didn't want to get you something you'd hate, so I've got you a gift certificate and I was hoping we could go together so you could pick something you wanted."

"A gift certificate?" Jamie couldn't hide the disappointment in her voice. She didn't want to shop at some stock standard boring department store style mass market jeweller. Not because of the money—she'd wear a ten dollar ring if that's all Amanda had—but because she wanted to support a craftsperson with a unique creation just for her.

"Um, yeah." Amanda pulled a small piece of paper out of her shirt pocket and unfolded it. It was a pretty piece of pink paper covered in scrawly writing. "I'm sorry. Doctor's handwriting."

Jamie squinted at the writing.

To Jamie. This paper promises you a ring of your choice to symbol our union. Amanda

"That's so adorable." Adorable? No, what Jamie meant was that it was perfect. A handwritten gift certificate promising her she could select her own ring from anywhere. She wanted to gush over it and hold it against her heart as if she were thirteen again. There was a jewellery designer in Melbourne who made the most adorable rings using uncut and rough cut gems, as well as some incredibly unique designs that were just... chef's kiss perfection. She bit her lip. Could she get a matching necklace with a locket that had a space for this note?

"So I guess this is official then." Amanda leaned back in the chair. "I should tell Ma and the girls."

"Now?" Jamie swallowed.

"May as well. I'll send Ma a text."

Jamie stared at Amanda blankly for a second—a text for such important news? She realised she ought to tell her parents too. This marriage was going to be real, at least on paper, and she should tell them before they found out via gossip. "Do you mind if I call Mum?"

"Sure." Amanda smiled. Jamie pulled out her phone and called Mum and wasn't at all surprised when she answered quickly.

"Darling. It's been days since we chatted. Where have you been?" Years after she'd quit modelling and moved home from the UK, Mum still had a hint of a London accent overlaying her North Shore Australian accent.

"I have some news."

"Good news. I could do with some good news. Did you know Jean-Phillipe cancelled my hair appointment this morning and—"

Jamie cut off her mother's usual rant about her pretentious faux-French hairdresser. She used to get her hair done by him, until she owed Stu an apology and instead went to Spiro's Barber Shop in Surry Hills. After the excellent job Poppy had done, she would never go back to Jean-Phillipe, and that was without considering the crappy way Jean-Phillipe had treated Poppy.

"I'm getting married."

"Craig? You know he reminds me of your father at the same age." Mum might not have meant to give Jamie nausea but that was the effect of her phrase. Jamie picked up her sparkling water and took a long sip to get rid of the sudden acidic taste on her tongue.

"No. Not to Craig."

"Oh excellent. He… well, now isn't the time."

"In other words, Father is listening."

"Yes. Now tell me all the details."

Jamie breathed in deep. At least with Father listening to Mum's side of the conversation, Mum wasn't going to react. "Her name is Amanda. She's a doctor."

"A doctor. Excellent. It's not exactly what I expected—"

Jamie rolled her eyes—knowing Mum couldn't see—at the way Mum phrased her reaction to the announcement she was marrying a woman. "I'm very happy, Mum."

"Good. And have you started thinking about any of the other details? Hold on. Your father wants to know why you are seeing a doctor."

Jamie couldn't avoid this forever and she braced herself for the conversation. "Put him on."

"Jamie. What is this about a doctor?"

"Father. This might come as a bit of a shock to you, but I've just got engaged." She waited for his censure.

"To a doctor?"

"Yes."

"We will need a new plan with regards to Craig and Kapow then."

Jamie sneered. "I blew him off when Kapow sacked him. You do realise he wanted to marry me because he wanted to own your business."

"I suspected, but I figured you would have that under

39

control. And I see you do… with your doctor. When are we going to meet him?"

Her. Jamie didn't say it, partly because she wasn't ready yet and partly because she was so stunned at his previous comment. "You assumed I had Craig under control and knew his motives?"

"Yes. You've always been good at reading people."

A compliment from her father was so rare that she nearly fell off her chair. "Thank you?"

"I'm going to hand you back to your mother. She will want to plan the perfect society wedding, I assume."

"Hello again darling. That sounded like it went very well."

Jamie reminded herself to breathe; maybe it had gone too well? "Yes, although he's assumed my doctor is a man. Will that be a problem?"

"Let me worry about that. If you are happy, then that's all that matters. You are my darling baby. I'd do anything to make you happy. You know that." Since when had her parents become all sentimental? "Now, have you set a date?"

"Not yet. How about I get back to you with that?" Jamie needed some space to process what on earth was happening.

"Of course darling. You'll need to ensure you decide quickly because the best venues are always booked out a long time in advance."

"Thank you, Mum. Bye." Jamie hung up and stared vacantly over Amanda's shoulder at the distance.

"You look puzzled. What happened?"

"Um, my father was nice to me. He complimented me and that's never happened before."

Amanda pushed her glasses up her nose and tilted her head a little bit. "I wonder…" She trailed off and Jamie leaned forward. Jamie realised that Amanda always held her head on that slight angle when she was about to say something profound and thoughtful. Her pulse sped up as she waited impatiently for whatever Amanda was going to say.

"What do you wonder?"

"Was the compliment after you announced our engagement?"

"Yes."

Amanda nodded slowly. "I wonder if he realises he's losing the control he had over you, so he's using a new tactic to keep you close to him." The cynicism was the perfect reminder that marrying Amanda was exactly the right choice.

"That's so manipulative—" Jamie sighed. "—and you know what, it's exactly what I'd expect from him. So yes, you are quite right. I'm sure that's what he's doing."

"You should be proud."

"Why?" Jamie blinked. Why should she be proud of her manipulative father? She didn't expect Amanda to side with him.

"Because you still have value to him, and he needs you."

"But why should I be proud of that?"

Amanda smiled, her face lighting up. "No, I meant you should be proud of you. Marriage means that he's about to lose his ability to control you, and if he wants to maintain that control, he has to find a new way to do that."

Jamie slid her phone back into her shoulder bag, then sipped her sparkling water again to give herself time to muse on Amanda's words. If she didn't trust Amanda's motives, she'd worry that Amanda was only complimenting her to get something from her. Could she trust Amanda? This marriage was a big commitment. But just as her brain began to stress on a loop, her baby fluttered in her stomach and suddenly all the doubts receded. Amanda was a doctor who understood how to vanquish Craig; and those qualities were exactly what she needed right now to give her baby the best chance at a good life.

"You know what Mum said? She said Craig reminded her of my father when he was young. I think that was a warning, you know."

"Quite likely. Fuck, when I met Craig I was so young and naïve. He seemed so confident and I was charmed by that, but the reality is that it was all ego and bluster with no basis."

"Confidence is very attractive." It was the main thing that drew Jamie to Amanda; how she held herself with the innate knowledge that her scheme would work, even though they barely knew each other. Jamie should question Amanda's reasons for doing this. Jamie carried a baby to Amanda's ex-husband; surely that was reason enough to sneer at her, yet Amanda had an openness that made Jamie query all her negative assumptions. Life had taught her not to trust other people. Why was she trusting Amanda now?

"It is." Amanda smiled and the mild uptick in Jamie's pulse calmed again. "I shouldn't be angry at my younger self for not being able to tell the difference between real confidence and fake egotistical confidence."

"It's funny, you know. I actually believe my Father's compliment. I shouldn't, but I do."

"What did he say?"

"He said that I was good at reading people, and I think it's true. I am good at reading most people. Well, everyone except my father, I guess."

Amanda nodded. "That will come with time and distance. People always reveal their truth eventually."

The waitress appeared at their table. "Excuse me, are you ready to order now?"

"Yes. I'll have the zucchini pasta salad." Jamie could do with some thinking space. She had a lot to ponder and it was hard to figure it all out while Amanda sat there so prettily with her intelligent gaze focused on her.

"I'll have the spinach and feta omelette. Thank you."

"I can't believe—" Jamie started.

"We should talk about the practicalities." Amanda spoke at the same time.

"You first."

"No, you."

"What do you mean practicalities? Like money. I have money." Jamie had her trust fund, but her father was also a signatory on that and she required the trust's—father—permission to withdraw funds. Would marriage change that? She pulled out her phone to make a note.

"I have a good job. I don't need your money." Amanda was either playing a long game here, or she truly did just want to stop Craig from inheriting Jamie's share in her father's business. Years ago, Jamie had set up her own independent accounts that her family didn't know about. All her earnings from her blog went in there, and she'd set it up so any withdrawal from the trust fund also diverted a portion to her own accounts. It was overly complex, but she'd slowly built up a decent nest egg in case Mum needed to leave her father's threatened abuse. They'd be able to achieve it safely because of her secret funds. So far she hadn't needed it because doing as she was told had kept Mum safe, and now she almost dared to hope that Amanda was right and it was all the threat so she would do as commanded. Had she become trapped in an endless cycle of obedience? Now was her best chance to bust free, ironically thanks to Craig's manipulations and the life growing inside her.

"Okay. I guess we keep our funds separate then?" If this marriage was to give her independence from her father, then Jamie wasn't going to immediately give that up to someone else. She held her breath, uncertain over how Amanda would react to the concept.

"Yes." The simple agreement, without any fuss, went a long way towards Jamie believing Amanda at her word on her reasoning for this marriage. "Did you want to move in with me? I know it's a big step, but you can pay me rent if that makes you feel more comfortable. Plus, you'll get to meet the kids and they can meet you before the baby arrives in June." Amanda paused. "I know it seems fast, so you can say no."

"No, I mean, yes. I'd love to move in if that's alright with you."

"I offered. Please move in."

"Will your children find it strange?" Jamie didn't know any children. She was an only child and so were her parents, so she had no cousins either.

"No, they'll be okay, kids adjust quickly to new situations. My Ma lives with us too. We can be a bit loud sometimes."

"Oh. Um, I'm sure it will be fine." Her stomach knotted. What if she upset one of the children? And what if they didn't like her?

"Super. Do you need any help with moving? I can get my cousins to help out if you need."

Jamie didn't know what to say.

"Am I going too fast? I tend to organise everyone in my life. Sorry."

"No, it's fine." Jamie needed to say something. "Honestly if you have an internet connection, then I'll be fine." *Fine, fine, just fine.* She wouldn't need to move many things, since she already paid for specialised storage for her clothing and jewellery collection. She'd spent years quietly preparing to move out of her father's home with no notice. She could throw a few things in a suitcase and she'd be gone.

"Awesome. Well, I'm on the evening shift tonight, so I'll be around all day until about four if you need me."

"But you ordered lunch. You aren't going to stay?"

Amanda laughed. "Of course I'm going to stay for lunch. Stop looking like a startled rabbit."

"Excuse me?"

"I'm sorry. Am I being too pushy?"

"No. It's fine." Again with the fine. "Can you please just give me a moment to organise my thoughts?" Jamie hated asking because it would remind Amanda that they weren't the same. Amanda was a doctor, she had to be super smart, and Jamie was… well, she'd always been terrible at school work.

"Sure." Amanda pulled out her phone and started reading.

"What are you doing?"

"I'm reading a book. You wanted time. Please take as long as you need."

"Seriously? Thank you."

Their food arrived and Jamie waited until Amanda started eating before she began. After a while, she put down her fork.

"What are your children's names?" Jamie knew nothing about Amanda's life, and she was about to step into a ready made family. A long way out of her comfort zone. What did she know about family except for manipulation and image protection?

6

Amanda's face softened. "I have two daughters. Madeline is six and Penelope is four."

"Those names are exactly what I'd expect Craig to call his daughters; slightly old fashioned, but trend setting. Feminine but not too girly sounding." Jamie cursed her loose tongue as Amanda's expression hardened at the mention of Craig, then an unexpected grin from Amanda had Jamie off balance again.

"You have no idea how much strategy went into these names."

Jamie relaxed a little bit, a mirror of Amanda's languid smile. "I'm named after my father. He's James."

"I was hoping you were named after that actress, Jamie Lee Curtis. She's so hot."

Jamie blinked. "Hot as in you are bisexual, or hot as in aesthetically pleasing."

"Jamie, I proposed to you." Amanda's flat tone didn't really answer her question.

"That was about revenge on Craig. We didn't discuss any…" Jamie's cheeks burned and she didn't know what to do next. Amanda sucked her bottom lip into her mouth and Jamie's face got even hotter.

"Most cis-het people I've met wouldn't conceive of a plan like this. I mean, yes, I'm delighted at the opportunity to stop Craig from winning with a shitty scheme, and I'm so fucking pleased to help you out of a bad situation. Our kids are siblings, they should grow up together."

"That doesn't… um?" She gritted her teeth against an impatient sigh. "You didn't really answer my question. Are you bi?"

"Yes. Yes, I'm bisexual. It's funny, you know, because it took me a long time to realise that everyone wasn't; but I guess that also means I'm lucky to never have to question myself. I think it's because Ma is too and she's always been open about it."

"Wow." Jamie tried to collect her thoughts, but she felt like she'd been electrocuted, and everything stopped working. She'd always swum around like a drowning kitten on this matter, never really knowing if she was valid in her desires or not. Most of the people she'd had sex with were men, and she wished she had the confidence in herself to know that it didn't make her less.

"And, I mean, fuck me. You are so beautiful, Jamie."

Jamie waved her hand dismissively. "Yes. It's my best asset." Just because she knew she was beautiful didn't mean anything about her. It was just her body and that was the main cause of her problems right now. Her body was a tool for others to use, a plaything for herself, and sometimes a joy, but right now she was just tired of only being seen as beautiful.

"Oh?" Amanda frowned. "I didn't expect you to say that."

"I'm not going to lie to you. I know I'm beautiful. It's a fact."

Amanda tilted her head and her glasses slid down her nose a little. "People don't often see you properly, do they? They look at your face and make assumptions."

"People do that to everyone. It's important to know your strengths and use them." Jamie parroted her father out of habit, then swallowed away the rising bitter taste in her mouth. "Mum was a model when she was younger, and she taught me how to sound humble without ignoring the simple fact that I'm aesthetically pleasing to look at. I don't see why I should pretend that I'm not pretty when it's obvious." And besides, she wasn't good for much else. Mum had stopped modelling after she was born, and heat prickled behind her eyes as a new worry added to her growing list. Once this baby came, her body wouldn't be the same and she wouldn't have any worth.

"Oh, I'm not asking you to pretend. It's refreshing to hear someone acknowledge their beauty and not pretend they didn't realise."

Jamie tried not to sigh at the assumption of confidence. She was just like all the other fashion bloggers and social influencers who knew how to get the benefit from their lucky genetics. "I think that often people aren't pretending they don't know how they look, but are actually trying to sound humble about something they didn't choose for themselves."

"Of course. Because women are always stuck with the impossible balance of being pretty enough to be noticed and not bragging about it because men like to be the ones who point it out."

"Something like that." Jamie wasn't keen on thinking too hard about this. "Can we talk about something else?" She had complex feelings about her looks; they were helpful and had made her a good amount of money, but she was literally in trouble—pregnant—because her father had used her pretty face for his advantage, and she hadn't been clever enough to see that Craig might also do the same. She was the one paying the price.

"I'm sorry. Does it make you uncomfortable to talk about it?"

"Yes." Jamie should've left it at that. "It didn't used to bother me, but now I find myself pregnant to a man I don't really like all to please my father, and…"

Amanda nodded. "I see. You feel manipulated and used. Did I make it worse by asking you to marry me?"

"Excuse me?" Jamie had spent a lot of time over the last week thinking about Amanda's motives and she understood exactly why she wanted to stop Craig from winning by deceit. "No. I feel like you've given me power." Getting married was her choice; and she didn't get to make many choices for herself.

"Good. I don't want you to feel like I'm pushing you."

"Not at all. In fact, let's do it today. We can go to a registry office now."

"I don't want you to rush into this. Marriage is a big step, we'll be tied together legally, and you hardly know me, so I want you to be sure."

"What about you? Are you sure?"

A slow smile stretched across Amanda's face, dragging all Jamie's attention to her lush mouth. "I've never been more certain of anything. It's probably the wrong motivation but I really want to beat Craig. He was such an arse to me for so long and yes, I'm using you to get one over him."

Jamie tried not to cringe as Amanda outlined her reasoning. It must have shown on her face because Amanda held up her hand.

"Wait. My motives have grown since I've met you. I've realised that I want more than revenge on Craig. I want to help you with your pregnancy and the baby. I like you."

The lick of desire that had chased up her spine at Amanda's grin flickered like a candle in a breeze, because Jamie wanted to believe Amanda actually liked her, and yet, people didn't usually see past her face and body. "No, you like the way I look."

"That too." Amanda grinned. The imaginary flame of desire burned a little brighter as Amanda's gaze darkened. If only she could revel in lust and ignore the reality of her situation.

"It doesn't count for anything. Craig is handsome and we both know how that worked out." Jamie hated feeling confused and she wanted to lash out at someone. Herself. Her father. Probably even Amanda, although every time she might, Amanda smiled and all her frustrations dissipated. Craig had been good in bed. Jamie liked sex and she refused to be ashamed of enjoying it even when she didn't particularly like him as a person. It was for mutual benefit; they both schemed for commercial reasons and got orgasms in the process. She wouldn't have slept with him more than once if it hadn't been fun, and she didn't regret it; at least not until she'd missed her period and it wasn't fun anymore.

"Very true." There was no satisfaction in seeing Amanda's smile disappear. "I'm sorry. What do you want?"

"I want to get married. I don't have the luxury of time." In a different situation, Jamie might have spent months figuring out if this was the right choice—weighing up all the options—but she was already starting to show and she needed security for her baby.

"Why not?"

"I'm already at nineteen weeks. Soon, this pregnancy will be obvious and I want…" Jamie really wanted a loving family for her baby, and Amanda might not love her but she obviously loved her children and that would have to be enough for now. Jamie was used to a life where she compromised what she wanted for others. This solution was a good option for her baby.

"Let's do it."

From the moment Jamie walked into the registry office with Amanda, to the point where they signed the papers committing to a life together, Amanda held Jamie's hand, and it cemented how right this was. It was the simple gesture of support, the notion that they were together in this choice, and the quiet flush of heat from Amanda's touch guided her forwards. Marriage would give her baby a family, some certainty, and it was a good solution to her problems. Besides, her father had heard the news and complimented her—sure, it was about something else—but it felt like he approved of her getting married. She wasn't going to investigate why she shouldn't still want his approval, when seeking it had led to this very place. Jamie signed with a flourish, impressed that they hadn't needed an appointment for the paperwork to create such a major change in her life.

"That's done now."

"You may kiss the bride," Amanda whispered, and Jamie nodded slightly.

"Yes." She leaned forward. Amanda rested one hand on her waist and reached up to brush Jamie's cheek with her other hand. The gesture seemed to pull Jamie down towards Amanda and she bent her head to kiss her. Soft lips touched and the whole room faded away. Gone were the glaring white lights and the sharp edges of the row of desks that the registry staff stood behind. Amanda's hand spread over Jamie's cheek and her mouth sang with her taste. It was a quiet, soft, gentle beginning of a kiss, one that promised more, one that hinted at a passionate joining, and yet it hummed like one of those piano solos that upmarket cafes played in the background. Jamie carefully wrapped her arms around Amanda's shoulders, and their bodies pressed lightly against each other. The shape of Amanda with her round tits and soft belly barely touched against Jamie's pregnant stomach and sharp hips and yet her whole body burned for more. Amanda parted her lush lips a fraction and their tongues met with a zing of mint and lust. Jamie's eyes flickered shut, she wanted to feel everything, and taste Amanda because this was a revelation of desire. Unexpected and incredible.

Someone cleared their throat and Amanda pulled away from the kiss.

Jamie opened her eyes. "Oh dear me." She'd forgotten where they were and that a stranger watched their first kiss.

"Good luck with the future. Your marriage certificate will be processed shortly and be posted to the address you supplied." The staff member's tone was filled with a sigh even though the words were clipped and efficient. "You make a lovely couple."

"Thank you." Amanda's cheeks were flushed pink and she pulled off her glasses and cleaned them on a little cloth. "Come on, let's go home."

"Home. Yes." Jamie let herself be led out into the bright sunshine of the street. It wasn't the summer sun that had her blinking though. "Um, I need to go and get a few things, and then I'll come by and settle in later. Is that okay?"

"After that kiss, I don't really want to let you go."

"Excuse me?" Jamie's thoughts hadn't caught up to the rampaging heat in her veins.

"I'm sorry. I thought the kiss was incredible and I want more."

"I want more too. Why are you sorry?"

"I'm not sorry. I guess I'm a little confused. I thought we were doing a marriage of convenience. Ha ha, and now all I want to do is drag you home to bed for more kisses. Is that too much?"

A wave of relaxation swept over Jamie's shoulders and she turned towards Amanda. Some of her hair had fallen out of her pony tail, and Jamie tucked it behind Amanda's ear.

"I liked the kiss too. I need to go and grab a few things if I'm going to stay at your place, that's all."

"Okay. You do what you need and I'll meet you at my place." Amanda stretched up on her tiptoes and pressed a short kiss to Jamie's lips. It was done before Jamie could react and she stood there with her mouth hanging open a little. Her lungs hurt a little and she realised she hadn't been breathing properly ever since they'd both signed the paperwork. She breathed in deep and smiled.

"I think this is going to get the start of something wonderful."

Amanda's smile stole all of Jamie's breath again. "I hope so too."

Jamie nodded before all her old doubts could trample on this fragile happiness. "See you soon." She walked down the street without a backward glance, because if she stayed any longer with Amanda, she'd never leave her side. And it was one thing to be married to someone who kissed like that—full of promise and passion—and quite another to give up her newly achieved freedom from her father so quickly.

7

Amanda had a skip in her step as she walked inside. The first step in her revenge against Craig was done. She was married, and yet it wasn't negative thoughts of retribution that filled her head. That kiss. Wow, shivers raced down her spine at the memory of Jamie's soft lips against hers. It'd quickly gone from a simple peck on her lips to a deeper connection and it had taken the gentle cough of the staff person to drag Amanda back into the real world.

"This is all my fault." It was typical of Ma not to bother with social niceties, like How was your day? And yet something in her phrasing immediately made Amanda's chest tighten.

"Why?" Amanda gasped, immediately focused on her children. "Who is hurt?"

"No one. Yet."

"Ma." Amanda growled a warning.

"Maddie and Penny are fine. They've finished their homework and are watching a bit of telly."

"So what exactly is your fault?" Amanda knew Ma did a good job with her kids; she'd been a solo mum as well and knew how tough it could be to juggle work and child care and everything else, but sometimes she could be a bit fucking vague.

"Your marriage of course."

Amanda shook her head and strode past Ma. Maybe now wasn't the time to tell her it was already a done deal. She went straight to the lounge and pulled her daughters in for a quick hug. "Good afternoon, my darlings. Did Grandma make you do homework?"

"Yes, but not much."

"They had to catch up on some things they missed while at karate yesterday." Ma had followed her.

"Mama, you are in the way of our show." Penny whined a little and Amanda smiled. She kissed her daughter on the forehead.

"Far be it for me to interfere with your important things." She walked to the kitchen, poured herself a wine, and turned to face Ma. "Now, please explain why my marriage is your fault."

"I wonder if I should never have sent you to ballet lessons."

Amanda's head whipped up and she glared at Ma. "What? I made so many friends there."

"But your friends are so heteronormative and traditional and I think you rushed into marriage with Craig because you wanted what they had."

Amanda breathed out. "Oh, you mean my marriage with Craig. Not Jamie."

"I don't want you to make the same mistake again. Just because your friends are happy with their lives and husbands, doesn't mean you need a husband to be happy. I'm happy with my choices."

Amanda had heard this song from Ma many times, how she didn't need a man to complete her, and being a feminist was about be able to make her own choices. "Just because you made your choices deliberately doesn't mean you don't regret them."

"Oh, I don't regret anything about my week with your biological donor. He had a magnificent… cee oh cee kay." Ma spelled out cock with a sideways glance at Maddie and Penny, who were so immersed in their TV show, they didn't notice. "And boy, he knew how to use it. But it was just a fun week on a beach, and even though I didn't expect to get pregnant, I don't regret that either. We've had fun, haven't we?"

"Yes Ma." Amanda knew the story of her origins and it was irrelevant to her situation now. "If all of that is true, why do you blame yourself for my marriage to Craig?"

"When you were young, you spent a lot of time at your friend's houses, and they had the whole traditional family unit thing going on. And I blame myself for not showing you that I was happy without that, that you didn't need to strive for what they had to be complete."

"Ma." Amanda didn't want to have this argument, because maybe an inkling of it was true. She had been flattered by Craig and how he'd painted a picture of a happy traditional marriage to her. Her best friend Arpana's parents had been a love match and Arpana's house was full of laughter with her three siblings. She had wanted that for herself; how Arpana's family supported each other in good times and bad. "You did the right thing, Ma. Please don't doubt that decision."

"I wouldn't be a mother if I didn't doubt my decisions. It's hard to see you grow up and make your own choices, and not know if I made a mistake in not guiding you away from hurt."

"Ma. You made the right decision." Amanda had long ago come to terms with never knowing her father—her biological donor as Ma called him—because Ma didn't know his surname or anything about him. He was a stranger that she'd fucked on a beach while on holiday. Together they'd created their own found family through the friends made at ballet lessons, at school, and at university, and they were closer and better than trying to include a random man whose only recommendation was that he was good at sex.

"I just don't want to see you go through all that awfulness with Craig again, especially if it's a misguided attempt to fill a hole in your life that doesn't need filling."

Amanda bit back a choking noise at Ma's accidental euphemism for sex. Accidental? Who knew with Ma; she'd never been quiet about how much she enjoyed sex. "It's different with Jamie. You'll see."

The loud knock on the door came at the perfect time. Amanda quickly gave Ma a hug. "You did a wonderful job, Ma. I'm happy." She stepped away, then rushed to the front door and opened it.

"Last time I stood here it was all wrong…" Jamie paused. A light flush covered her cheeks and Amanda wanted to know if it was because of their earlier kiss, or simply caused by the memory of Jamie's confrontation.

"And now it's perfectly right. Please come in."

Jamie stepped inside the house, lifting her small suitcase over the doorstep, then bent down and slid off her elegant sandals. Amanda held her breath as she closed the door behind Jamie, trying and failing not to stare at Jamie's long legs.

"Ma is keen to meet you."

"Oh." Jamie pressed her hand to the base of her throat. "I'm so nervous. Do you think your children will like me?"

"This isn't really about liking though, is it?" Amanda wished she could haul the words back inside because Jamie's eyes flicked open wide, then she stared down at the floor. "I'm sorry. This is new for me as well."

"Okay." For Jamie to accept her half-assed apology only made it worse. Somehow she'd become caught up in the drama and thrill of getting married and had forgotten that Jamie had zero self-esteem. She would have to be careful that Ma's forthright nature didn't crush her. Or her own, to be honest.

"Come on." She reached out and grabbed Jamie's hand. A sharp prickle of energy flew up her arm and she wished she could be like Ma and simply just kiss her without worrying about everything else. Instead, she walked towards the kitchen. "Ma. I want you to meet someone. This is Jamie."

Ma's mouth gaped and Amanda winked at her.

"Hello. It's lovely to meet you."

"And you too, Jamie. Welcome to our home. And Amanda?"

"Yes?" Amanda grinned, waiting to see what Ma would say.

"I take it all back. I'm sorry I didn't trust your decisions."

"It's fine, Ma. You had good reasons." Amanda glanced at Jamie. A frown marred her face and Amanda realised that Jamie would think all the wrong things about what Ma had said. "Come on, Jamie, let me show you around the house." She held Jamie's hand and virtually dragged her from the kitchen and along the hallway towards the bedrooms. Once inside her room, she turned to face Jamie.

"I'm so sorry. Ma assumed I was getting married to a man, and she went on and on about how I didn't need a man to complete me, and how she blamed herself for my apparent need to have a heteronormative marriage."

"A what?"

"You know, like man and woman."

"Right? Doesn't she like me?"

Amanda had to stretch up to kiss Jamie on the cheek. Jamie was rather tall with her long model worthy legs. "I'm so sorry."

"It's not your fault that she doesn't like me."

"No, that's not true. Ma probably does like you. I'm sorry that I was annoyed at Ma assuming you were another Craig, and I didn't tell her about you. I'm sorry that I used your arrival to shock her."

Jamie stepped back, opened her mouth, then closed it again. Amanda waited and the pause was worth the wait.

"How often do you make decisions for petty reasons?

You married me to get revenge on Craig. You didn't tell your own mother that I was a woman because she annoyed you with an assumption. What will happen when I do something you don't like? Will you play this game with me?"

Amanda staggered backwards and sat on the edge of the bed. Jamie may as well have slugged her in the face with her fist for the way her words cut at the heart of every decision Amanda had made. She'd become a doctor because a teacher at high school had said she couldn't. How had she not realised this about herself until now? Was she just a petty bitch motivated by revenge? Were any of her choices truly hers?

"Honestly, I don't know. You don't have to stay with me. We can just have the marriage on paper if you want."

Jamie shook her head. "I'm not sure."

"You'll always be welcome here. I'm going to make that promise to you. I realise it probably means nothing in the light of my behaviour, but I want to hold myself to that promise and keep my house as a safe space for you."

"Okay."

"Jamie. I know it seems all a bit sudden, but please know that you are welcome here. I want you."

"Can you stop talking?" Jamie stepped towards her, knelt on the ground before her, and kissed her. "I believe you, Amanda, and I want more kisses too."

Amanda nodded, more than willing to park any introspection until later. Later, she'd have to dwell on how uncomfortable Jamie's observation made her feel, but right now, Jamie's lips against hers stole away her ability to think. She cradled Jamie's face and dipped her head to kiss her again. Jamie's breath whispered over her lips and a hint of mint cooled her heated lips. She pressed her lips against Jamie's, caving to her need for more, and knowing that as she kissed her, she wanted to prove herself. This marriage wasn't just petty revenge. It might have begun that way, but now Amanda wanted Jamie for herself and she poured everything into the kiss to show her. Light touches, followed by a deeper kiss when Jamie opened her mouth. The entirety was intoxicating and when Jamie pushed herself up to stand, Amanda followed, with her legs squeezed between Jamie and the bed. Her arms stretched up, still cradling Jamie's gorgeous face. Oh fuck, she was so beautiful, and so blasé about it that Amanda didn't want to say anything in case it was dismissed. She wanted to complement the way Jamie listened and discovered information about her, things she hadn't wanted to admit.

"You are so clever, my beautiful wife." Amanda breathed against Jamie's cheek, as she let her hands drift down Jamie's long neck to rest on her shoulders.

"I don't need to be lied to. I want to bed you."

Amanda frowned. "It's not a lie." She tried to step backwards so she could hold up her hand in a wait gesture, but fell backwards onto the bed. "Oof." They both giggled, and Jamie lay down beside her.

"I know I'm not clever. I almost failed high school, and I studied so hard."

"Clever isn't always about academics. You are so good at judging people, at reading their emotions, and seeing what they want."

Jamie raised one elegant eyebrow. "I'm literally pregnant because I failed to do that."

"Do you always dismiss everything positive about yourself?"

"No. I have a beautiful face and good bone structure. It's a saleable face."

Amanda gritted her teeth. "Even that is a dismissal. Your face is beautiful. It's also worth more than its ability to sell products. You shouldn't value yourself on external measures."

"How else do I value myself?"

"By your own internal strength and I know you have lots of it."

"You do?" Jamie looked at her with wide eyes, hanging on every word with a hope that slayed Amanda. She had to work to drag a smile out and appear relaxed because that was what Jamie needed now. Reassurance.

"Yes. Look at you. You didn't give up when the worst thing happened to you. You found me—"

"Yeah, that was not my best idea."

"Looks pretty great from here." Amanda leaned forward and kissed Jamie on the tip of her nose. Jamie cringed, then giggled.

"Why?"

"Because I want to be with you. I want this to be a real marriage, not a scam to best Craig at his own game. I—" She couldn't articulate it; the knowledge that she was falling in love with her wife. "I like you Jamie and I want to kiss you until you cry with joy."

"Please. I would like that."

Amanda needed no more encouragement and she kissed

Jamie deeply, seeking her tongue, as she ran her fingers over Jamie's slender neck, down her throat and further down to the neckline of her sundress. She didn't need to glance down to know the dress would be tangled around Jamie's long legs, maybe taut around Jamie's rounded pregnant stomach, only now starting to show. She traced one hand down Jamie's side, over her waist and hips, stretching as far as she could and yet not quite reaching the end of her dress. Amanda bundled the fabric in her fist and dragged it up until finally, Jamie's skin was exposed for her. She shifted on the bed, sliding her lips over Jamie's sharp collarbone. Jamie moaned, a gentle breathy hum, then twisted and suddenly Amanda found herself deliciously, perfectly, trapped underneath Jamie.

"Oh. I like that."

Jamie loomed over her with heat in her gaze and pressed her into the bed, her weight only momentary before she pushed herself up on her hands, creating an angle where her dress clung to her tits and gave Amanda the ultimate view down her cleavage. Someone moaned and Amanda realised it was her. She tugged her hands free and slid them up Jamie's waist to cup her tits.

"What about this?" Jamie thrust her hips against Amanda with a flirty glint in her eye. This was the Jamie that Amanda adored, when she was confident and assured, and Amanda wanted to see Jamie become this person all the time. Imagine. She was already wet from Jamie's weight on her, and when she rubbed her thumbs over Jamie's hard nipples, she felt herself buck. All it took was a good pinch, and Jamie gasped.

RENÉE DAHLIA

"You have too many clothes on." Jamie unbuttoned the blouse Amanda wore, and with every single button came light touches against her skin that made her want more. It took all her effort to focus on pleasuring Jamie's tits while she was distracted by Jamie's fingers stroking the skin down her torso. Jamie rolled them together on their sides and pushed Amanda's blouse wide open.

"You need better lingerie."

"I do?"

Jamie ran her finger across the cup of Amanda's bra, then up the strap and plucked it gently, so it stung her skin. She groaned and she wrapped one leg over Jamie.

"This is so functional, and you are very pretty. Let me buy you something nice. Something beautiful."

Amanda could only nod as Jamie took charge, stripping her of her clothes, efficiently and yet with careful thought, until Amanda lay on the bed, naked and so utterly teased that her brain stopped working. Jamie knelt beside her with her feet near Amanda's head and kissed her on the stomach, then dragged her lips lower and lower until Amanda could do nothing but anticipate.

"I'm clean." She managed to croak out the words as Jamie pushed her thighs wide, and blew cool air over her clit. "Oh fuck yes. Like that."

"Such a dirty talker." Jamie sounded amused and Amanda half sat up, confused for a moment.

"Excuse me?" Amanda had painted Jamie as slightly helpless and needy in her mind and it seems she was completely wrong.

"There's something you need to know about me, Amanda." Every word created a huff of breath on her wet pussy and she struggled to do more than nod.

"Hmm, what?"

"I love sex. It should be obvious, given my condition. I love it and I want to kiss you. There." Jamie stretched her long arms out and grabbed Amanda's ankles, slowly dragging her hands up Amanda's legs and every inch of her caresses had Amanda panting for more. When she held Amanda's thighs, pressing them wide open, and leaned in for a kiss, Amanda flailed her hands in Jamie's general direction. She needed to touch her too, and Jamie knew it. She shifted closer to Amanda, with her pert arse in the air and her sundress hanging over her legs, tempting. Amanda flicked the fabric up onto Jamie's back, and the sight of Jamie's bare arse with a simple yellow strip of fabric—her g-string matched her dress—as the only barrier between her and heaven was almost too much. She gripped Jamie's leg and tried to shift it so she was being straddled. Fortunately, Jamie knew what she was doing, and moved easily. Amanda's vision filled with wet pink pussy, surrounded by neat hair all clipped short. Amanda pulled her closer, needing to taste. There was nothing tentative about this anymore, she desired Jamie more than anything, and she was desperate to touch, to taste, to know her. Just as she readied herself to lick with her tongue, Jamie sucked on her clit and she cried out. Fucking hell. Desperation ruled, her hips bucked, and she stretched up to lick Jamie. Her musky salty taste filled her mouth as she exploded. The dual sensations in her mouth and in her pussy were too much for her thudding heart, and she almost stopped to ask if she was being too rough as she licked and sipped at Jamie's core. Her fingers dug into Jamie's soft thighs—damn, her skin was so incredibly soft and smooth—and she stopped thinking. Just sucked and fucked with her tongue while Jamie did the same to her. Pressure and tension built in a delicious buzz that skittered across her skin until she exploded with it, coming harder than she'd ever done before. She slid two fingers inside Jamie, holding on as she convulsed and cried with the sheer joy of her release, and just as her orgasm started to fade, Jamie came, leaning back against her hands and mouth, urgent and clenching hard. Taste exploded on her tongue, so delicious. Jamie's thighs shook and then she rolled slowly sideways, collapsing beside Amanda with one leg draped over her collar bone. The heaviness of her limb felt completely right, as if Amanda had finally found her home.

"You are incredible and I never want to hear you doubt yourself again."

Jamie chuckled and kissed her on the top of her curls. "Sex makes you so fierce."

Amanda blinked. "Just for you." She wriggled out from under Jamie and twisted around so she could kiss her on the mouth again. Jamie's minty breath now tasted salty and amazing with the remnant of her own orgasm on Jamie's lips. She felt like addicts must when given a hit of their drug of choice; she wanted more and more of Jamie, never wanting to leave this bed and worry about anything else. They lay there, entirely wrecked and relaxed, in each other's arms for ages. Amanda lost track of time and space, simply allowing her body and mind to enjoy the aftermath of being with Jamie. A loud knock interrupted her nap and she growled under her breath. Jamie's gentle laughter sent a breeze over her ear; the absolute best way to wake up.

"Love birds, it's time for dinner." Ma called through the closed door.

"Ma! We'll be there shortly."

"Does she know?" Jamie's sexy confidence disappeared, and Amanda could almost feel the emotional wall being built in record time.

"That we've been fucking? Yes. But don't stress. Ma is a free spirit. Now, let's go and meet Madeline and Penelope." She kissed Jamie on the forehead and dragged herself off the bed to fix her clothes.

8

Three weeks later, Jamie groaned as Amanda's alarm went off. She wriggled against Amanda's warm skin, still unable to believe her luck. After the initial nervous negotiations, they'd spent all their spare time in bed together and the sex had been explosive. Amanda said that it was her pregnancy hormones, but Jamie knew better. It was all Amanda. She'd never had orgasms as strong as the ones with Amanda and her clever fingers. Last night, they'd gone to sleep entangled with each other. Again.

"Isn't it your day off?" Jamie wanted more sleep before today's big meeting.

"Yes. I thought we could go for a walk at the beach this morning."

"Are you serious? I mean, the girls will probably love it, but I have to get ready for today." Jamie wanted to look perfect when she introduced Amanda and Ma and the girls to her parents. There would be no reason for her parents to criticise her, or rather she would give her parents nothing to complain about.

"You have hours to do that." Amanda rolled over and pressed Jamie into the mattress. She wriggled, not because it was uncomfortable, but because she needed to prepare for today. Her parents were going to meet Amanda today. They were all going out to lunch together—deliberately in public to prevent ugly emotional scenes—and Jamie wanted it to be perfect. When she'd agreed to Amanda's plan, she could never have imagined this life. Maddie and Penny had leaped into her heart as if they were her own daughters, and she was slowly getting accustomed to Ma's outrageous sense of humour. Ma had the same whippet-quick smarts as Amanda and their conversations flicked from topic to topic. Amanda brushed her lips over Jamie's mouth, ending her ability to think. She kissed her back, and gently rolled onto her side, so her body pressed gently against Amanda's without her weight against her pregnancy. Tomorrow she'd be twenty-two weeks, past half way and her baby was moving more frequently now. She traced her hands over Amanda's side, down past her waist and over her hips.

"I could wake up this way every day."

"You do." For three weeks now, they'd woken up tangled in each other and continued where they'd left off the night before. Amanda's hands stroked over Jamie's skin as if she were precious and Jamie wished it were true. During the day, and sometimes at night, Amanda went to work where she oversaw babies being born and helped save women and their babies when a birth went wrong. The whole idea was so miraculous to Jamie, and yet, Amanda hardly talked about her work. Was it because she didn't want to worry Jamie about her own pregnancy?

"Stop thinking."

"How do you know?"

"Your hands stopped moving." Amanda winked, then slid her hands down Jamie's spine and grabbed her on the ass. "You are starting to round out with the pregnancy." Her hands squeezed, and slowly slid between her thighs.

"Are you saying I'm getting fat?" Jamie shouldn't care but she heard Mum's voice in her head. She would have to go for a longer walk today. Jamie wasn't ready to examine how her parent's obsession with her looks had made it impossible not to worry about how her body was going to change. So much of her worth was wrapped up in looking good for their image; and it had been so relaxing not to spend so much time focused on it lately. No one in Amanda's house cared if her face was made up or whether her hair was brushed. Yesterday Penny had complained about getting her hair brushed and had threatened to shave it all to save her the bother. Ma only agreed with her and said that it would grow back. Jamie stepped in and offered to brush it and the smile on Penny's face was brilliant. She adored Amanda's children. This past three weeks had been like living in a happy bubble and now it was all about to pop.

"Jamie. You are supposed to be getting plumper. You need the energy to feed your baby. And besides, all this stress about body image is just society talking. It doesn't matter."

Jamie frowned. "What do you mean? You are fit and healthy." She ran her hands along Amanda's side, and her fingers touched the rough stretched skin from Amanda's own pregnancies.

"I focus on staying healthy for the sake of my heart. How I look is irrelevant provided my body works as I need it to."

"Well, I like the way you look." Jamie would rather kiss Amanda than keep stressing about what her parents were going to say about her at lunch today. She shifted so she could cradle Amanda's face in her hands and she kissed her with every snippet of passion she could summon, all adding up into a fury of desire. More slow burn than flashy explosion and exactly what she needed to get out of her headspace. Amanda's kisses were the best, they had a possessive energy that made Jamie feel special, as if each kiss was reserved just for her. Amanda hands wandered as she kissed, and when she cupped Jamie's breast, Jamie sighed into Amanda's mouth.

"We are going to be late." Jamie's toe jiggled on the floor of Amanda's car as she parked on a side street not far from the restaurant. "We shouldn't have gone to the beach this morning."

"The beach was so fun," Madeline called out from the backseat.

"The girls really needed the run to take the edge of their fidgets and if we didn't go, you would have spent the morning worrying about lunch." Before Jamie could protest, Amanda turned off the car and twisted towards the back.

"Now girls, remember, best behaviour. We are going to meet Jamie's parents and I want them to think you are well behaved children."

"It sounds boring." Penny whined and Jamie wished that would be true.

"If you are good, I'll buy you an ice cream afterwards," Ma said. The two girls squealed, and Jamie grinned. She placed her hand on Amanda's shoulder.

"Come on, let's go before we are more than fashionably late." Jamie pushed open her door and stepped out onto the footpath. She wore a flowing dress that wrapped in a cross over her boobs; it helped contain them now they were spilling over the top of her bra. Soon she'd have to get a bigger cup size. Gah. She'd chosen this dress because it hid all her secrets from her parents. It was nerve wracking enough that they were meeting Amanda and her family, without them knowing she was pregnant. Hopefully they'd just think she'd put on a little weight; something in itself that would cause enough comments.

"Stop stressing. I'm sure Ma will hold her tongue and your parents will like me and the girls." Amanda's Ma laughed, having clearly overhead her daughter.

"Easy for you to say."

Amanda wrapped her arms around Jamie's waist and rested her head against Jamie's arm. Her presence comforted while also reminding her of exactly what was at stake here. "I should be the most nervous one. I'm about to meet my highly judgemental in-laws who are bound to hate me."

"Why? You are a doctor."

"And a woman. How many times have you told me that they care about their image?"

"My father is in advertising. He's seen everything and he knows how to sell it. He'll tell the world his daughter-in-law is a doctor and an amazing human and that'll be it. No one would dare to contradict him."

"If that's true, why are you nervous?"

"Never mind. Let's go." Jamie knew it was her they would judge, not Amanda, but she couldn't stress about that now they were running late. She peeled herself out of Amanda's hug and stood up straight. She checked her make up in the car mirror, touched up her lipstick, then walked towards the restaurant. After letting the staff know they were there, she blew out a few long breaths to slow her unsteady heartbeat.

"Please come with me." The maître d' led them into the restaurant towards a table. Her father sat with his back to them, Mum to the side, and there was one other person at the table. The man glanced up. Craig. All the air in Jamie's body left as if vacuumed out.

"Father. Mum. Craig? What are you doing here?"

"Oh, it's the biggest coincidence. I have the table beside you booked and I'm early for a client meeting."

Beside her, Amanda scoffed under her breath, and Jamie didn't dare glance at her. Coincidence? No, Craig never worked like that. He'd figured this out and was here deliberately. Dickhead. Worming his way into her father's good graces; she had to stop worrying about what he might have said before she'd arrived. She swallowed and lifted her chin higher.

"Jamie." Her father stood up and kissed her on each cheek in his usual perfunctory manner. "I invited Craig to join us. I hope you don't mind."

"I do mind, actually. This lunch was for you and Mum to meet my fiancée, not to talk business with an ex-staff member."

Craig's jaw tightened. "Fiancée? I thought—" He paused for the tiniest moment before switching to a different tack. It was so typical of him that Jamie barely bothered with a shrug. "Advertising is a small world. I've been lucky enough to secure a position with Dunstable and George. I was simply talking shop with your father."

"And now you can leave. This is a private family gathering."

"I'm family."

Jamie shook her head. "No. You'd like to be, but you'll find that position has been taken by someone far superior to you. Please, I'd like to introduce my wife, Dr Amanda Aitken."

The stunned look on Craig's face as Jamie stepped aside to reveal the people standing behind her was worth everything she'd sacrificed until now for her father's corporate manipulations. Perhaps there was something fun to be had in Amanda's notions of petty revenge. As it was, Amanda recovered first.

"I'm so thrilled to meet you Mr Cleveland and Mrs Cleveland." Amanda ignored Craig.

"Daddy." Madeline and Penny rushed past Jamie and Amanda towards Craig. "Do you have any sweets for us?"

"No because I promised your mother that I wouldn't do

that." Craig glared at Amanda. "You. How did you meet Jamie?" Anger filled his eyes, and it was only a slight raise of eyebrows from Jamie's father that seemed to hold the tense moment in check.

"Craig, please excuse us. This is a family matter."

"And it seems I'm part of this family." He placed his hands on his daughter's shoulders.

"Now is not the time or place for this discussion." Ma stepped in front of Jamie. "Come along girls. Say goodbye to your biological donor who has missed his last three weekends with you." The nasty little backhander didn't even make Craig flinch.

"I've been busy."

"Too busy for your children? Then you won't miss them today either. We'll get an ice cream and be back later." Ma held out her hands for the girls and they jumped up and went with her. As she was leaving, Ma exchanged a glance with Amanda and Jamie knew there would be a long argument later. One she would try and diffuse because this was all her fault, Amanda had nothing to do with it bar the same taste in terrible men.

"Well, that could have gone better." Jamie started but it was Amanda's contained rage that filled the air.

"What in the absolute fuck do you think you are doing here Craig? I refuse to meet my new in-laws with my ex in the room. Leave." She used the same quiet tone that owned the room that she'd used on the day Jamie had turned up on her doorstep.

"Did you steal my girlfriend just to get back at me? How pathetic."

Jamie held her breath as Craig hit on the truth.

"I love her. It's more than you could offer her. It's obvious that all you wanted was to con your way into a business. You've never been good enough to create something for yourself. Always sliming your way into success via bludging off other's people's hard work." Amanda still didn't raise her voice and yet everyone listened to her.

"I think that's enough now." Jamie's father cut through the argument. "Craig, we can discuss work at another time."

"And so now I'm dismissed? You've stolen my children and my home, and now my fiancée. I hope you are happy." Craig stormed out of the restaurant and everyone breathed out. Jamie's breath caught in her throat; she had never been Craig's fiancée and yet she couldn't manage to get the protest out.

"Please sit down." Mum waved to the table and Jamie's father sat down.

"I'm sorry you had to see that disagreement with my ex-husband before I've had a chance to introduce myself. Unfortunately, Craig didn't cope when I was promoted at work and began to earn more than him. He's found it hard to adjust to parenting his daughters on the occasional weekends when he takes them."

"When you run in a social circle as small as ours, you are going to meet the same people, and not everyone can manage past relationships appropriately. It says a lot about you that you stayed polite when he made such accusations of you." Mum had always been adept at managing awkward social situations. She really was in her element at Father's side, and it astounded Jamie that their relationship in private was so much more contentious. Not that she'd ever seen them fight, but they both spoke about it. Jamie blinked; had they both made up any abuse to keep her obedient? Now was not the best time to realise she'd been lied to by both her parents for years. Heat prickled behind her eyes and she blinked hard to stop any tears from falling.

Jamie's father patted Mum on the hand. "Not many people are as blessed as us in their marriage, my dear."

The false portrayal of their happiness jolted Jamie out of her shock over Craig's revelation. Amanda had been upfront about wanting revenge on Craig, but to hear him say it so outright reminded her that she'd said the same thing to Amanda only yesterday. Had the whole three weeks of their marriage been a lie? The sex had been better than with anyone else and Jamie assumed it was because they'd had a really strong connection, that sex with Amanda was more than just bodies combining. To Jamie it had felt like a meeting of hearts. Was she wrong? What she wrong about everything?

"Can you please stop with the pretence that everything in our life is perfect? You've spent years forcing me to be your business spy and holding threats over me." It was becoming obvious to Jamie that no one was going to tell her the truth. No one would look after her and her baby except herself. She needed the truth. Now.

"Jamie, my darling daughter. You've always had a wonderful imagination." Her father managed to make it sound like she'd made up every threat he'd made. The earlier heat in her eyes became a stabbing red hot poker and her body felt emptied out. A shell of a person and she couldn't stop the doubt filling her mind. Maybe he was right and she had invented all of it?

Father leaned across the table towards Amanda. "She gets that from me, you know. If she'd been better at school, she'd already be my right hand lady at the office."

"Jamie doesn't need to be good at school. She is beautiful." Mum ran her critical gaze over Jamie. "That dress looks incredible, a good selection for your frame, although you've certainly put on several kilos lately. You'll need to be careful that it doesn't become more; weight is so hard to shift once it's on. And have you been doing your skin care? You have the right bones to age gracefully."

"Yes, Mum." Jamie's reply came automatically, while inside she faded a little more.

"One thing I've learned about marriage is that you require a partner who compliments you. Your mother is elegant and knows how to talk to our wealthy clients and make them comfortable. That will always be worth more to me than youth, although, my dear, you do have spectacular bone structure and are as beautiful to me as you were when I met you."

Amanda glanced sideways at Jamie, a tiny frown hiding under the rim of her glasses. "I'm incredibly lucky to have Jamie in my life. My daughters love her and so do I. We came here today hoping for your approval and blessing for our union, but I've come to realise that we don't need it. Jamie is enough for me as she is. When she is old, she will still be herself and that's all that matters to me." Amanda's hand brushed her thigh under the table, and Jamie grasped it. She needed it like a lifeboat from a sinking ship. Did

Amanda understand that her father had just lied about everything? And why did Mum agree? It was all so unsettling, especially because she wasn't sure of Amanda's role in all this either. She felt like she was standing at the top of a sand dune, and the ground was sliding under her feet, changing and slipping, dragging her downwards as she scrambled to stay upright at the top of the dune.

"Jamie will always be beautiful, even in old age, because she is like her mother. My question was really about you. You already have one failed marriage under your belt." Father didn't pull his punch and Jamie felt it in her solar plexus.

"Provided Jamie doesn't cheat on me or lash out in jealousy when I earn more than her, then I think we will be fine."

Father smiled at Amanda's retort as if he approved of her. "It's brave of you to blame your failed marriage on Craig when he is someone I know particularly well." Father didn't bother to hide his sneer and Jamie wished he'd just stop, although it was satisfying knowing that Amanda would see the falseness in him.

"Let's not talk about that now. Have you set a date?" Mum once again eased the tension by changing the subject, and finally Jamie knew how Mum could both be like this in public and keep up the charade of potential abuse in private. It was the same mechanism.

Jamie stood up. "Excuse me for a moment." She rushed away from the table towards the toilets. Amanda could scheme with her parents without her listening. Oh damnation. This whole marriage was a terrible idea—she'd merely swapped one manipulating jailer for another. When Amanda proposed she'd said she wanted revenge on Craig and she didn't care about gaining access to Father's business but seeing them together showed her that it was a lie. Everything was a lie. Amanda clearly outwitted her in the cleverness stakes and she could hold her own against Father. Jamie knew him well enough that she could see his approval—the approval she wanted for herself—in his eyes when he spoke to Amanda. If anyone met his impossible standard, it was Amanda and she must have known that she'd outshine Craig for the role of heir. She locked the cubicle door and plonked down on the toilet seat. What now?

9

Amanda had never experienced anything like lunch with Jamie and her parents. The whole thing reeked of toxicity in a private school polite way that scratched at her skin. It took all her effort not to thump the table and drag Jamie away from them. When Jamie had first mentioned her father threatening her with abusing her mother in order to keep Jamie in line, Amanda's first instinct had been to believe her. She just hadn't realised how insidious the situation was. Jamie's parents were too united for there to be one-sided abuse; it was likely they both emotionally abused and gaslit Jamie. She was a tool for their business ambitions, not loved for herself, and it hurt Amanda as if she was the one being harassed.

"Thank fuck that is over. I think we need to set some very strong boundaries around spending time with your parents." Amanda paced along the waterfront towards the playground with Jamie at her side. They'd farewelled Jamie's parents and waved as they got into a fucking Bentley and drove off.

"Perhaps."

"Yes. Definitely."

"Okay." Jamie sounded exhausted, and for good bloody reason too. She sat very still—rigid—during the rest of lunch, nodding politely, and not offering much in the way of conversation.

"Come and sit here with me for a moment. The girls are fine with Ma, she sent me a text only a few minutes ago, so we have time." Amanda tugged at Jamie's hand and walked towards a bench seat overlooking the water. Several families played in the sand and on the water's edge with happy squeals and giggles, and Amanda allowed herself to get distracted for a second with the notion of watching her own daughters swim here. The shark net surrounding the bay gave everyone the notion of safety too. Amanda waited until they were both seated, then turned to Jamie and held her hands.

"Remember a few years ago, there was a shark attack here. It made the front page of the paper, and the guy showed off his leg with a few streaks of blood running down it."

"Here? But there is a shark net."

"Yeah. I remember the whole thing because it was bloody ridiculous. It turned out to be a wobbegong."

"Seriously?" The tension radiating off Jamie eased and she almost smiled.

"Yeah, the guy had a few scratches on his leg from their tiny sandpaper like teeth and the whole thing was completely overblown." Amanda hadn't had a plan when she'd started this story, only that she wanted Jamie to relax after such a stressful lunch. "Jamie, I'm really sorry. I had no idea Craig would be there, and I overreacted to his presence. I know I said I'd marry you to get petty revenge on him, and that's a common pattern in my life. One that I'm going to work on trying to notice more so I can change."

Jamie's mouth stretched into a slow smile, and Amanda's heart skipped a beat.

"I understand the enjoyment you get from petty revenge. It was quite sweet today. No one has ever defended me quite like that." Hearing that from Jamie's lips only added to the desperate need Amanda had to make things right for Jamie. What she needed was to be loved unconditionally with no one making decisions for her. She needed to choose for herself and Amanda wanted to empower her to do it.

"Being with you is sweeter than any notion of revenge. I'm glad Craig brought us together, because marrying you has been the best decision of my life. It doesn't matter how it started. I want to carry on with you. I love you."

"You do?" Jamie frowned.

"I do. I really do. You've had a harder road in life than many people would assume when looking in from the outside. It's obvious that your parents colluded with the abuse story so they could control you. It's emotional abuse, and I'm—" Amanda closed her eyes and breathed in and out a couple of times to quell the way her chest clutched tight. "—I believe you and I love you."

J amie gulped. She wanted to believe Amanda more than anything in the world. "Can you please give me some time?"

"Absolutely. It's been a rough day."

Jamie nodded. She felt battered by today's lunch and to have Amanda state so clearly that her parents had worked together to keep her working for them was a revelation she didn't feel she was ready to accept. This was going to take a lot of time and a bloody good therapist.

"Come on. Let's go and hang out with Maddie, Penny, and Ma in the playground, then we can all take you home for a rest."

"I don't need to be doctored. And I certainly don't need to be told what to do." Jamie had spent her life being told what to do, and it'd never been with her best interests at heart. She—selfishly—wanted to put herself first for a change. Whatever that meant.

Amanda brushed her finger across Jamie's bottom lip. "I can't promise not to doctor you. It's what I'm trained to do, but you have to know Jamie. I love you as you are. I think I loved you from the moment you stood on my doorstep, all vulnerable and brave, apologising for Craig's dickhead behaviour. I would never tell you what to do because it would destroy the joy I get from seeing you choose for your-self. I'll always be thankful that you chose me."

Jamie breathed in deeply, and the sea air filled her lungs. "I did choose."

"Yes."

"I made a choice, and that choice is you, Amanda." Jamie couldn't get rid of the doubt filling her brain; that would likely always be there. She could choose Amanda and she could choose this family they had together. The last three weeks had been the best of her life, just living together in harmony without any demands from anyone. She'd had coffee with Vince and Riley, she'd spent time with Poppy talking about marketing her hairdressing business, and she'd worked on her fashion blog. She had chosen Amanda and it was the best choice she'd ever made for herself.

"Take me home, Amanda. I'm yours." Jamie needed rest more than anything, and to sleep in Amanda's arms sounded like heaven. Everything she needed was at Amanda's home; a family who adored her and people who cared for her. No one in Amanda's family used her for their own gains, they just accepted her completely. Amanda's acceptance and her love was the best gift she'd ever been given. Together they could make a family and both Jamie and her child would be safe and happy.

EPILOGUE

One year later.

Amanda walked in the door after another long shift at the hospital and the sound of laughter surrounded her. There was something so wonderful and energising about a home filled with happy people.

"Mum, Mum." Penelope skidded to a halt in her socks on the wooden hallway floor.

"Yes?"

"Tracey said her first word and I knew we should have called her Bibi."

Amanda laughed, all her work worries fleeing at the reminder. "Bibi is too close to baby."

"Her first word was bibi." Penny stood with her hands on her hips, and a righteous look on her face. "Tracey is too hard to say, anyway. Why did you pick it?"

"Mama liked it and it means brave. I think Mama was super brave to join our household of feisty girls." Amanda pulled Penelope into a hug. After a long discussion with everyone, they'd decided to stick with Ma for their girl's grandmother, Mum for Amanda, and Mama for Jamie. Having two mums and a grandma was better than anything, according to Madeline.

"You are silly, Mum. Come and listen."

Amanda let herself get dragged inside to listen to nine month old Tracey gurgle. She held up her favourite toy, a squishy truck, and said, "Bibi."

Jamie leaped to her feet and kissed Amanda on the cheek. "Welcome home. Penelope has spent the last month trying to get Tracey to say Bibi and she's achieved it."

"Her first word."

Madeline scowled. "Not true. She said Ma yesterday."

"That doesn't count. Saying Ma isn't a real word, it's just what we always call everyone."

"Hey, it must be time to help me set the table. I'm sure Mum doesn't want to hear you all bickering after a long day at work."

"It's fine. I'm always happy to be home with my family. I love listening to all of your chatter." Amanda took off her shoes, wriggled her toes, picked up Tracey for a cuddle, and sat down on the couch. This was the life she'd always wanted. A job that interested and challenged her, and a partner who loved her and supported her in her endeavours. Jamie had grown in confidence in the last year thanks to a lot of therapy and love. Once they'd worked out that she had dyslexia, she'd really thrived and now Tracey was old enough to be left with Ma for a few hours at a time, Jamie had started to work part time at Cleveland Marketing with the aim of taking over when her father wanted to retire. Amanda hadn't been sure about Jamie's choice to stay involved with her father's business, but she wanted Jamie to make her own choices and she would support her regardless of what happened. The best she could be for Jamie would be to be here for her if or when something went wrong, and to support her freedom to choose, and most importantly to celebrate when Jamie succeeded.

Craig was still a distant father who reluctantly paid child support for his three offspring; but life was never perfect and honestly, Amanda was still petty enough not to want him to find complete happiness. She'd learned not to react to every situation with a plan for revenge and it was probably Jamie's love that helped her outgrow that aspect of her personality. She channelled it into competitiveness now, which was a lot more positive than seeking retribution for every slight against her. She'd never regret wanting to beat Craig because she wouldn't be here right now without her plan to beat him, but it had all settled in her mind into a much healthier positive frame of mind.

"We love having you home." Jamie glowed, and Amanda grinned at her wife and lover.

"I'm so lucky to have a wonderful wife and a happy home filled with three amazing daughters."

"Don't forget Ma."

"I wouldn't dare!"

Jamie paced across the room to stand beside the window and cleared her throat. "I have some news." Whatever the news was must be big, given the way she nervously twisted her hands together. Amanda wanted to wrap her in a hug and reassure her that they could work it out together.

"What is it?" Maddie asked.

"You know how we've been joking about how my father's business should be renamed Cleveland and Daughters, because he's only got me, and all of us now."

"Yes?"

Jamie shook out her hands. "So... I've been working on being brave with my therapist, and I did it."

"What did you do?"

"I asked Father and he said yes. It's official. Cleveland and Daughters will be launched... relaunched... next month."

Amanda couldn't contain her squeal of joy and she leaped off the couch, holding Tracey nice and tight, as she bolted across the room to wrap her very clever, gorgeous, wife in a hug. "Congratulations. That's massive and I'm so proud of you."

"I love you, Amanda. I couldn't have done it without your support and your belief in me." Their hug was made even better when Maddie and Penny joined in. This was the life she wanted. This was the life they'd created together.

ALL BOOKS BY RENÉE DAHLIA

Thanks for reading HER PREGNANT RIVAL. I hope you enjoyed it. Reviews can help readers find books, and I am grateful for all honest reviews. Thank you for taking the time to let others know what you've read, and what you thought.

If you'd like to know more about me, my books, or to connect with me online, you can visit my webpage www.reneedahlia.com and if you sign up to my newsletter, you can grab a free book Ode to the Banh Mi.

Twitter https://twitter.com/dekabat

Facebook https://www.facebook.com/reneedahliawriter/

Instagram https://www.instagram.com/reneedahlia_author/

You've just read a book in my Kapow series. The other books in this series are:

1. Out of Her League (fm with bisexual characters)

2. Rekindled (ff) Short Story (also included as a bonus in Out of Her League)
3. His Buxom Beauty (fm)
4. Craving His Spotlight (mm)
5. Her Pregnant Rival (ff)

If you liked this book, here are my other books:

Contemporary Series: Farrellton Foster Family

1. Betrayed (fm)
2. Liability (ff)
3. Forbidden (fm with bisexual characters)

Contemporary Series: Merindah Park

1. Merindah Park (fm)
2. Making Her Mark (fm with bisexual heroine)
3. Two Hearts Healing (fm)
4. Racetrack Royalty (fm)

Contemporary Series: Rainbow Cove

1. His Christmas Pearl (fm)
2. His Christmas Pride (mm)

Contemporary Series: Homage

1. Ode to the Banh Mi (fm with bisexual heroine)

2. Uplift (ff with bisexual heroines): Only One Bed anthology (KU)

Historical Series: Great War Ladies

1. Her Lady's Honor (ff)

Historical Series: Bluestockings

0.5 The Shipwrecked Earl's Bride (fm with bisexual hero): 12 Rogues of Christmas anthology (KU)

1. To Charm a Bluestocking (fm with bisexual hero)
2. In Pursuit of a Bluestocking (fm)
3. The Heart of a Bluestocking (fm)

www.ingramcontent.com/pod-product-compliance
Lightning Source LLC
Chambersburg PA
CBHW070630120726
47909CB00004B/1378

9780648962632